Grilled Sand and Witches

A WATER WITCH MYSTERY
BOOK FOUR

LEAH R CUTTER

KNOTTED ROAD PRESS

Grilled Sand and Witches
A Water Witch Mystery
Book 4
Copyright © 2024 Leah Cutter
All rights reserved
Published by Knotted Road Press
www.KnottedRoadPress.com

Cover Art:
GetCovers.com

ISBN: 978-1-64470-409-7

Cover and interior design copyright © 2024 Knotted Road Press
http://www.KnottedRoadPress.com

Reviews
It's true. Reviews help me sell more books. If you've enjoyed this story, please consider leaving a review of it on your favorite site.

Come someplace new...
Are you a traveler? Do you enjoy exploring strange new worlds, new cultures, new people?

Sign up for my newsletter and I'll start you on your travels with a free copy of my book, *The Island Sampler*.

http://www.LeahCutter.com/newsletter/

Buy More!
Did you know that you can buy directly from the Knotted Road Press website?

https://www.knottedroadpress.com/shop/

Also by Leah R Cutter

War Among the Crocodiles

The Cassie Stories

Poisoned Pearls

Tainted Waters

Spoiled Harvest

Bloodied Ice

Epic Fantasy Series

The Fallen Elves

Ruins of the Gods

Stairs of the Gods

Cities of the Gods

Graves of the Gods

Houses of the Dead

Houses Divided

Houses Fallen

Houses Reborn

Forgotten Gods

A Wind Blown Torment

A Stone Strewn Clash

A Sea Washed Victory

The Tanesh Empire Trilogy

The Glass Magician

The Desert Heart

The Ghost Dog

Science Fiction

The Long Run

Project Nemesis

Project Nyx

Project Tisiphone

Project Persephone

War of the Allied Worlds

The Labors of Darius Linard

Huli Intergalactic: Science/Space Fantasy

Origins

The Strawberry Girl

Chapter One

AJ walked casually across the lobby of the Bridgewater Inn. She had plenty of time before her meeting with the folks from the Left Coast BBQ Association (LCBA), and planned on stopping in at the Storm Brew Café to pick up a sandwich on her way there.

The lobby hadn't changed much in the almost two years (two years!?!) since AJ had arrived in Milltown. Beautiful marble black-and-white checkered tiles covered the floor. Antique chandeliers made of glass blown there on the Washington State coast graced the high, two-story ceiling. The white paint still looked fresh, though AJ suspected that they'd have to redo it in a year or so.

All the changes had happened behind the scenes, as it were. Rosita and her family now owned the inn. In the reception area, where Willow was currently working, instead of an ancient behemoth of a desktop taking up space, there were two sleek notebook computers that accessed a modern reservation system.

Though AJ still only worked part-time, she was hoping to cut down her hours even more come fall. It wouldn't be fair to do it now, during the busy summer season. Particularly since she wasn't quite ready to full support herself as a psychic.

AJ had almost made it to the stately wood-and-brass doors that opened up onto the front courtyard when someone called her name.

"AJ? AJ Steward?"

AJ contained her sigh and instead, plastered a pleasant smile on her face. She'd made it a point to *not* spend her life grabbing meals between meetings anymore, but sometimes it couldn't be helped.

"Yes?" she said, looking around to see who'd called her.

A tall Asian woman approached her. It took AJ a moment to place the woman, since seeing her here was so out of context.

"Lili?" she said, stepping forward. She remembered at the last minute not to hold out her hand for a handshake. Lili didn't like touching other people, not if she could help it. Something about not just making her uncomfortable, but also germs.

"You remembered," the young woman said, putting her hands behind her back.

Lili stood a touch taller than AJ's own five foot ten, and they shared the same slim, athletic build. She was first generation Korean, with a flat face, eyes so dark you couldn't see the pupils, a tiny nose and thick lips. Her black hair hung down past her shoulders, the ends scraggly, not a curtain of satin. She wore her usual uniform of a light peach T-shirt and black jeans. Wearing the same colors of clothing left her with fewer decisions that she had to make in the morning, as she'd once explained.

Lili had been one of the developers AJ had managed a lifetime ago, when she'd worked at a small tech startup in Seattle. Before AJ had retired, her life had imploded, and she'd ended up here in Milltown.

It was difficult to get a grasp on Lili's emotions as she tended to speak in a monotone and used so few facial expressions. AJ assumed that Lili was glad to see her, and was just as happy that AJ hadn't reached out to touch her.

"Are you here for the BBQ competition? The Milltown Open?" Lili asked.

"I live here, actually," AJ said. "I manage this inn."

Lili blinked for a couple of seconds, processing the information.

"The inn is one of the sponsors for the competition," Lili said slowly, her entire posture stiffening.

"That's correct," AJ said, nodding.

"Can I be seen speaking to you?" Lili said, her tone shifting enough that AJ could tell she was worried.

"Yes," AJ said after a few moments, finally figuring out what Lili was talking about. "I'm not a judge." The inn did have a block of rooms set aside for the judges who'd come in for the weekend, as well as the LCBA members who'd traveled there for the contest.

"Good," Lili said, nodding, possibly relaxing a shade. "That's good."

"Are you here for the Milltown Open?" AJ asked.

"I am," Lili said. "I retired a year after you did, about

the time I started doing BBQ competitions every weekend."

"Will you be staying here? At the inn?" AJ asked, a little confused. Didn't most of the competitors stay in the official campgrounds, with their gear?

"Only tonight," Lili confirmed. "I always get to a site early and treat myself to a night in a hotel before I have to *camp*."

AJ suppressed a smile at the emphasis that Lili placed on the word camp, as if it were a horrid task she had to perform.

"Don't care much for camping?" AJ said.

"It's so dirty, and dusty," Lili complained. "It's impossible to keep every surface clean."

"I see," AJ said, not too surprised at Lili's comments. She was something of a germophobe. "I'm on my way to a meeting," AJ continued, "but I wish you the best of luck in the competition." She'd have an opportunity to visit the competitor's campsite later, as well as sample some of their BBQ. She was looking forward to trying Lili's. If nothing else, all the health codes would be followed to the letter by her camp.

"Thank you," Lili said. "I have a good chance of winning this contest," she stated blandly. "I'm using two custom-configured barrel smokers, with extra fans, controlled by a Raspberry Pi."

AJ was certain that all those words were in English, though she didn't quite understand what Lili was saying. "That's good?" she said.

Lili nodded. "The computer—the Raspberry Pi—

monitors the temperature and controls the fans, so I get a much more even smoke on my meats."

AJ couldn't help but grin. Of course, Lili would be using computers to help her cook. AJ had met a few of the other contestants, most of whom used much less technology.

Then of course, there was Gabby, who was a fire witch, who controlled her smoker using magic...

"I'd love to catch up some time," AJ said.

"After the competition," Lili said, sounding serious. "I need to stay focused."

"Sounds good," AJ said. "See you later."

She knew she had to escape quickly, or Lili would go on (and on) about what appeared to be her latest passion since she was no longer working as a developer.

AJ finally made it out of the inn and into the beautiful May afternoon, happy the forecast said that the nicer weather would hold for all of the Memorial Day weekend.

The front of the inn was immaculately trimmed, the rose bushes edging the grand, circular driveway already starting to send out a few scented flowers. In another couple of weeks, the place would be heady with the scent, one of the reasons why AJ loved this place so much. A few lilacs were blooming as well. Green grass filled in all the empty spaces, already losing its spring brilliance, but still a welcome sight after the dreary winter.

AJ hurried along the street, past the round-about at the end of Main Street and down to the Storm Brew Café. She had just enough time to pick up her sandwich before her meeting.

After that, she was free for the rest of the afternoon.

Free to spend more time with Gabby, learning about water magic, as well as magic in general. Then maybe spend some time catching up with her boyfriend Roland.

AJ didn't see any clouds on the horizon, either literally or figuratively.

Hopefully, it would stay that way.

Chapter Two

AJ reminded herself that she was *not* about to smack Bob Woodard, the LCBA's contact person.

No matter how tempting it was. No matter how much he might deserve it.

She tried not to allow his looks to color her opinions of the man. Sure, he might have a pale pasty complexion that came from being indoors all the time, or possibly from living under a white hood. That recessed chin of his gave him an unfortunate ferret-like appearance. His hair was also receding, and his blue eyes were frequently icy. That mustache did him no favors either, looking as though a fuzzy caterpillar had crawled up onto his upper lip and died.

Honestly, though, it was his voice that bothered her the most, a nasal tone that made everything sound as though he was either being insulting or whiny.

"But what about the trophies?" he was asking.

"They'll be here," Sandy assured the man once again.

AJ was so happy that Sandy Gerlach, owner of the Milltown restaurant Sandy's Grill, was the person in charge of the Milltown Open committee, and the town's point person for the LCBA. Sandy's no-nonsense approach had saved their butts more than once, particularly with Bob.

Sandy looked like one of the old-time fishermen who lived on that part of the coast. Her cheeks were always red from being out in the sun and wind, her close-cropped blonde-gold hair fading into white, her meaty hands frequently banging on the table during whatever meeting she led to make sure everyone was paying attention. She wore comfortable flannel shirts over her very ample figure, along with jeans that had seen better days. She often tromped around town in crabbing boots.

AJ had offered the woman free psychic readings as a result of her leadership on the committee. Plus three free nights at the inn for any of her friends or relatives.

Sandy had yet to take AJ up on either offer, but AJ still hoped that Sandy would consider it at some point.

She might not, though, as she was that independent type who didn't believe in "charity" or some such nonsense.

It wasn't charity, at least not as far as AJ was concerned. Sandy was made of spitfire and gold. It was an awesome combination, and just what this organization had needed.

While AJ had never wanted to grow up to be her own mother—too locked down and controlled—Sandy could be considered a good alternative role model.

"And what if the trophies aren't here in time?" Bob whined.

"Then I will personally drive up the coast to Sunshine, the next big town, and pick up a bunch of trophies on my dime," Sandy said, glowering. "Satisfied?"

Bob pressed his lips together, looking as though he wanted to complain some more, but he seemed to discover some level of self-preservation, so he let the matter rest.

"If that's it, then this meeting is adjourned," Sandy said, using her hand as a gavel.

Before AJ could escape and get back to her place, where she was going to be meeting Gabby, Bob cornered her.

"Ms. Steward? A word?" he said, beckoning her to the side.

AJ maintained her pleasant "the customer is always right" smile as she approached.

"What can I help you with, Mr. Woodward?"

Though Sandy always made a point of calling him "Bob," AJ tried to be more appeasing. At least at this point.

"What are the chances that we'll be able to get the Bridgewater Inn to cater the next meeting of the LCBA?" Bob asked.

"I don't know," AJ said honestly. "It's going to depend on when the meeting is and how many people are attending."

She wasn't about to tell him to go someplace else, though a part of her wanted to. Payne Thomas, the chef in charge of the inn's café, was a committed vegan. He'd accidentally taken a person's life when he'd been younger and out of control, drunk and on drugs. Now, he had a religious fervor about the food he cooked that always made AJ a little uncomfortable. Despite him being the most handsome man she'd ever met.

Unfortunately, he didn't have a good palate, always coming up with dishes that were near inedible if she let him have his head. Plus, he might have *ideas* about what to serve an organization dedicated to cooking and eating meat.

And while Bob Woodward might be an asshole, the rest of the LCBA didn't deserve to suffer.

"A dozen people," Bob said, "the day after the competition."

"Monday night?" AJ hazarded.

Bob nodded.

AJ considered for a moment, then decided to be honest with the man. "The café is generally closed on Monday nights, to give our staff some time off. It's always the slowest day of the week."

If he checked the website for the inn, something that AJ personally kept up to date, he'd see that clearly spelled out.

"That would be perfect, then," Bob said. "As you won't be busy."

AJ shook her head. Obviously, Bob had no concern for anyone other than himself. Hadn't she just clearly stated that the staff got the time off?

"I don't believe we can accommodate you for food,"

she said firmly. "What you could do is work with the Storm Brew Café. They could cater the event, and you could still hold your meeting in one of the inn's meeting rooms."

The inn had an agreement with most of the restaurants in town, allowing them to come in and cater events held in one of the conference rooms on the second story of the inn.

Bob sighed. "I suppose you want me to set up the meal with the café, myself," he whined.

"It will be a lot less expensive if you do it that way," AJ said honestly. The restaurants tended to charge the inn more for the food if they ordered directly, than if the customer came to them.

"What, you won't be hosting us for free?" Bob sputtered.

AJ blinked, surprised. "No?" she said. She shook her head. "You can have the conference room. I won't charge you for that. But the food must be paid for."

She could already hear Rosita complaining about the extra expense of cleaning the conference room without being paid.

However, if the Milltown Open went well, AJ hoped that the LCBA would hold many more events in their area. There was already talk of doing a second event that fall.

"Fine," Bob said, turning away angrily. "Just see if we'll do business here again."

AJ contained her sigh.

At least Bob wasn't the only member of the LCBA

that the town business committee dealt with. While he might make it unpleasant for them, the rest of the association had been more relaxed and easy-going.

AJ hoped that she hadn't just ruined the town's chances of additional competitions.

It wasn't her fault. Bob Woodard was just an asshole.

Chapter Three

AJ sat with Gabby in what she called her reading room—where she did all of her psychic readings for clients. It was one of her favorite rooms in the old Craftsman house that she'd bought from Ursula, her mentor. AJ had agreed, as part of the sale of the house, to start a psychic business and run it out of her house, as her mentor had.

AJ had completely redone the room, painting the walls a soothing blue-green color while freshening up the ceiling with bright white paint. Graceful seashell-shaped sconces filled the room with a soft light. The old table in the center of the room was the same one that Ursula had used, made from oak with beautifully carved legs and sides. Though AJ no longer covered it up with a tacky purple tablecloth.

AJ's scrying bowl sat in the center of the table, an elegant hand-blown piece with swirls of blue and green circling the sides of it. A crystal pitcher filled with clean water stood to the side, given to AJ by her sister Bea. The now-worn tarot card deck that AJ had been using for readings since she'd started her business sat on the other side of the bowl, still snuggly encased in its black velvet bag.

Gabby had asked AJ to fill her scrying bowl sot that they could work on AJ's farsense, as Gabby called it.

Gabby was younger, shorter, and much rounder than AJ. Her dark skin and eyes proclaimed her Mexican heritage, as did her long, straight black hair. She wore brightly colored clothing—tonight she was in a turquoise blue T-shirt with a black-and-white checkered long-sleeved shirt over it, and black and white leggings that had images of cats dancing across them, all of them in bright red-and-green bowties. The long braid going down her back had pink and peach colored fake flowers woven into it. She also wore much more makeup than AJ did, with bright red lipstick and dusky pink eyeshadow.

At first, AJ had been shocked to discover another witch on her doorstep, willing to teach her about magic.

They'd spent most of that first afternoon getting to know each other, talking of magic and showing each other what they could do.

Gabby had been impressed at how AJ could manipulate water, being able to mold it like clay, create a shield with it, or to splash it out like a fist. She had the same level of control with her own element, fire, producing dazzling light displays for AJ to admire.

While AJ's visions almost always involved the future, Gabby's were about the present and where she needed to go next. It was the reason why being part of a BBQ competition team made so much sense for her. It gave her a good excuse to go from one town to the next, dealing with the supernatural elements there before moving on to the next place.

Fortunately, Gabby's sister, Cecilia, and Gabby's girlfriend, Elanor, were happy to tag along. The three of them formed the BBQ team *Las Chicas de Carne,* while the rest of their family ran a BBQ truck down in San Francisco with the same name.

As far as AJ had been able to determine, the teams may or may not break even on any particular event. While there was some prize money, it wasn't that much. Particularly since the team had to provide all the meat they cooked for a competition, which could get really expensive.

Instead, the BBQ competitions were more about advertising for the teams' restaurants or food trucks. Frequently, companies that sold BBQ accoutrements—such as grills or accessories—attended the competitions, and winning teams could snag a sponsorship. In addition, competitors hyped their own merchandise, as many sold lines of rubs and sauces, both at the contests as well as online.

Maintaining an even heat in a smoker was a key component of a team's ability to win. Gabby was the fire mistress, as the other two members of her team referred to her. She stayed up all night tending the fires on their smoker when the competition called for it.

She also dealt with whatever supernatural thing that needed to be addressed in that area.

Though AJ was still uncertain if she could trust Carla, the ghost of another psychic who'd died the previous year, Gabby had assured her that Carla had come to Gabby in her dreams, directing her to the town of Milltown and to AJ in particular.

That was part of what Gabby referred to as her farsense, the ability to sense what people were doing from afar.

She insisted that AJ had a similar ability, even though AJ's psychic ability, so far, had been primarily limited to being able to see the future. She'd been able to peek into the past a couple of times, but only with the help of a ghost.

Tonight, they were working on AJ's farsense again.

And failing, as they had been all week.

AJ was aware that some psychics could see into the past, and that her inability was psychological as much as anything else.

Her past wasn't the best place. She didn't want to go revisit it. Instead, her gaze was firmly focused on the future.

Maybe, though, she could expand what she saw to the present. Gabby had compared her own farsense to being able to see using her peripheral vision instead of just a small, tunnel-vision area of straight ahead.

So they tried again. AJ's scrying bowl was filled with crystal clear water from the pitcher that her sister Bea had given her. Though sometimes the water sat in the pitcher for a few days between readings, the water always remained fresh and pure.

AJ didn't think there was anything magical about the pitcher, that instead, the water was reacting to her presence. Gabby agreed, as all fires, even those she wasn't focused on, tended to burn cleaner and better around her. Some people in the BBQ competitions vied to get a space beside their camp. Others, though, considered her crew bad luck, as they weren't used to such hot fires and would end up burning their product instead.

Generally, to prompt a vision, AJ found herself falling into some sort of chant. It didn't have to rhyme, but it did have to be easy to say. They'd been trying the same technique with her farsense.

That night, AJ had made up a nonsensical poem about seeing the town, just to try something different.

> *O bright Milltown*
> *Shining by the sea*
> *Show me what's around*
> *Everything to see*

She felt stupid saying it out loud, as well as happy that her younger sister Bea wasn't there listening and giving her the usual hard time.

For a moment, AJ felt hopeful. Fog appeared on the surface of her scrying bowl, swirling in winds she didn't feel.

Then it dissipated, leaving her with a clear surface again.

"Did you see that?" AJ asked Gabby.

"I didn't see anything, no," Gabby admitted. "I did feel something, though. There was a pull in the air. The smell of rotten fruit being cooked."

AJ looked at Gabby quizzically, but she just shrugged.

"I think something's going on, but it doesn't have to do with me," she explained.

AJ blinked, surprised. Their magic, while similar, as they were both elementalists, was still very different.

She tried again, repeating the verse a few more times.

Nada.

AJ sighed, sitting back in her chair, frustrated. When she took a deep breath, she felt something there. Something lurking just under the waves. It wasn't the strong pull that occurred when she had a vision pending. Instead, it was just a slight current tugging at her. A gentle pull instead of a strong undertow.

She shook her head, pushed herself forward again, and then started speaking. She wasn't really aware of what she was saying, just something that stuck in her head.

"Show me the contest. Show me the meat. Show me what's going on. Show me the meat. Show me. Show me."

She felt herself lulled into a trance as she repeated the words over and over again.

The top of her scrying bowl filled with fog briefly, then cleared, leaving behind a silvery, mirror-like surface.

Slowly, a green color started tinting the water, creeping in from the sides until the entire top of the water was no longer silvery.

AJ held her breath as something started rising from the depths of the bowl.

It was a face. A face with a receding hairline, as well as a receding chin. The mustache he sported seemed alive, squirming across the man's upper lip. Prominent cheekbones stuck out under sunken eyes.

AJ found herself dropping a stone into the water before the apparition could open its eyes. She didn't need to see them to know that they'd be solid white, no color or life left in them.

She shivered, turning to Gabby.

"What is it? What did you see?" Gabby asked. "I saw a bit of mist, but that was it. And the smoke—well, the smell of smoke was definitely rotten."

AJ drew a deep breath before she spoke.

"I saw Bob Woodard. Dead. Poisoned, I think."

Gabby's eyes grew wide. "Was that in current time? Or the future?"

"Future," AJ said. "But he's a dead man walking." AJ's visions showed either a symbol representing a person, which meant that the future wasn't set, or the actual person, which meant that it was.

"We need to go warn him!" Gabby said, standing.

AJ nodded, agreeing, though she knew it wouldn't do any good.

They raced out of the house to Gabby's car, then down Main Street toward Sandy Point and the BBQ competition campgrounds. Though AJ had assumed that Bob would have taken advantage of the relatively inexpensive room at the inn, he'd instead chosen to camp in his fully decked-out RV.

However, the flashing lights of the police greeted them at the entrance to the campgrounds.

Bob Woodard was already dead.

Chapter Four

Fortunately, the pair of them had a good excuse for pulling into the campgrounds, namely, that Gabby needed to return to where she was camped.

Though AJ didn't want to lie to the police, she also *really* didn't want to tell Officer Brendan or Officer Naomi about another vision.

There wasn't anything they could learn at the campsite, so Gabby just turned right around, insisting on driving AJ back to her house, not letting her walk back up Main Street on her own.

AJ could tell that Gabby was shaken. She was certainly more upset about the man's death than AJ was. She wasn't about to say, "Good riddance," to Bob Woodward. He might (might?) have redeeming qualities that she'd been unaware of.

Maybe. Somewhere.

"Are you going to be okay?" AJ asked as they neared the end of Main Street.

"I've known of Bob for years, before I got into

competition. And I've also known him personally for quite a while as well. It's just...I can't believe he's gone. You know?"

AJ nodded. Though her last boyfriend, Ken, had cheated on her, and she'd been the one to cut him out of her life, it was still similar enough to a death that she recognized the feelings Gabby had.

"I'm sure the police will figure it out," AJ said.

"I'm not so sure," Gabby said. "You had a vision about it."

AJ couldn't contain her sigh. Yes, she had.

There had been other deaths in Milltown since AJ had arrived, as well as other crimes. No more than usual, according to Bea. In fact, there had actually been another murder just that past winter, two young men killed in what eventually turned out to be a drug deal gone wrong. However, AJ had never had a vision about it. Had never been in touch with the police about it. For some reason, her visions only occurred for crimes where she should be involved, not every crime that occurred in Milltown.

"You're right," AJ said slowly. "I probably am involved, and need to stay involved."

Gabby nodded as she drove around the traffic circle at the end of Main Street, then pulled off to the side to park. "Are you going to be okay tonight?"

"I'm fine," AJ assured her. "I had very few dealings with the man, and none of them were that pleasant."

Gabby snorted. "Yeah. He wasn't, like, the best person. Still, I didn't want to see him dead."

"Do you have any ideas who could have done it?" AJ asked.

"There are far too many suspects," Gabby admitted. "No one liked him."

"That means our work is cut out for us," AJ said seriously.

"You get some good sleep," Gabby said. "We can talk more about this in the morning."

"Okay. Goodnight," AJ said, exiting the car. She started walking down the short incline toward her house that sat on the beach. The night was cold, and swaths of fog rolled across the ground.

Before AJ reached her house, her phone pinged.

Roland.

With a smile, AJ answered. "Hey, you," she said.

"I heard the news about Bob Woodward," Roland said. "Just wanted to make sure you were okay."

"Thanks," AJ said, touched that he'd called. She let herself into her house as she kept talking. "I did have a vision about him."

"Oh?" Roland said. "Could you have saved him?"

"No," AJ admitted. "He was already dead in my vision."

"I see," Roland said, sounding resigned. "Do you need food? Company? A night cap?"

AJ smiled. Roland had finally come to understand that offering to help was useless. Actually making suggestions of comforting gestures was much more useful.

She paused, thinking. She and Gabby had had a good dinner, with Gabby providing an *amazing* prime rib while AJ fixed them a salad. Though AJ had had a glass of red wine with their meal, Gabby had abstained, as she rarely ever drank. Something about how alcohol and fire didn't mix.

Did AJ want something more to drink? Did she want company?

"I think I'd just like to chat for a while," AJ said honestly. It was one of the many, *many* things that she liked about Roland, that he didn't automatically assume that they needed to be in the same space all the time.

Sure, it was nice to have a body around, someone to cuddle with. However, they were both adults who had their own busy lives. When they got together, it was a choice, not the default.

AJ put Roland on speaker while she went into the kitchen and stuck her head under the sink there, getting her short hair completely wet. Bea thought she was weird for wanting to dunk her head in the water that way, but AJ had put in a large farmer's sink when she'd remodeled the kitchen just for that purpose.

After she wrapped her head in a towel, she poured herself a nice cup of soothing decaf chai tea before walking up the stairs to her bedroom, listening to Roland the entire time talk about his day, then the book he'd been reading, something to do with immigration patterns to the Pacific coast during the 1800s.

Finally ensconced in her bedroom, AJ was able to add more to the conversation, telling Roland about seeing Lili that day, the unpleasantness of Bob Woodward, and all the little things that had happened.

Slowly the conversation rolled to a natural end. They promised to stay in touch before they said goodnight.

AJ sighed as she got herself ready for bed. Roland was

a good boyfriend, nice to date, and willing to move as slowly as she wanted to.

Sometimes, though, like that night, she had the impression that he'd like to move things along further, for them to have more of a commitment to one another.

It wasn't as if she was about to go off and date someone else. Really, it was a small town and the pool of available (and desirable) men wasn't very big.

Not a problem for her to solve that night though. She was more than happy for them to have a slow-growing attraction rather than rushing into anything.

Besides, for her to make a commitment, she'd have to tell him about her magic. He knew about her visions, but she hadn't taken that further step yet.

That felt too final, and she wasn't ready for it.

Would she ever be ready?

That was a question for another day.

Chapter Five

Despite no official word from the police, the next morning the Milltown app—which served as the best news site in the area—was full of gossip on how Bob Woodard had been poisoned. He'd been throwing up just before he passed out, and some reports were that his lips and his fingertips were bright blue.

That Bob had been poisoned made sense to AJ, particularly given the shade of green that her vision had showed.

Had she actually seen the future, though? Or had she seen the present, and watched Bob Woodard dying? AJ wasn't certain. All she knew was that his death had been inevitable. And not just because the man was an asshole.

There was an emergency meeting of the Milltown Open committee that morning, trying to make the decision on whether or not to continue with the competition or if they should postpone.

The consensus was that postponing would mean losing a lot of sponsorship money, goodwill, as well as income from the event, as they'd probably end up refunding so many tickets.

If Bob Woodard had been a likable person, perhaps the vote would have gone differently. However, it was unanimous that, "the show must go on."

AJ left the meeting and hurried down Main Street to the inn. The people working the front desk had covered for her that morning, understanding that she had to miss work due to the unusual circumstances. The inn was an absolute madhouse when she walked in, the lobby filled with people, the line almost out the front door.

She didn't bother going to her desk but instead went directly to the reception area and started helping Willow and Sooli out, checking people in and getting them situated.

Two hours later, a familiar face finally walked up to the reception desk. Roland Jax, her boyfriend, carrying coffee. He wore his standard yellow-and-black-checked flannel shirt over a clean white T, sturdy dark-brown workpants, and heavy duty boots. His brown hair was cut short, with flecks of gray gracing not just the temples but all across his head. He'd look very *distinguished* when it had fully come in. His beard was well-trimmed, and his brown eyes shone with warmth.

"Bless you, thank you, bless you," AJ said reaching across the desk for the nectar of life. As the line of people waiting to check in had dwindled, Willow had left. Sooli shooed AJ away, saying that she could handle it for now, until the Friday afternoon rush started.

AJ walked out from behind the reception desk, tasting the coffee. It had a sweet undertone that she couldn't figure out, along with a touch of cinnamon. Steamed milk, and was that nutmeg as well?

"Do you know what this is?" AJ asked with a smile.

Roland shook his head. "Barista special," he said with a grin.

AJ smiled up at Roland, who looked as warm and solid as ever. She couldn't help but lean in and kiss his cheek. He smelled of wood and grass. He'd mentioned the night before that he'd be working all morning. The busy time for his lawn care business had started up in February, planting spring flowers for some of the businesses as well as doing the winter trimming. Summertime would be crazy busy for him, but then, come fall, it would calm down and he'd have a few months to read history and do research.

"I think she said it was apple pie?" Roland said as he snaked an arm around AJ's waist, giving her a kiss on the cheek as well.

AJ took another sip. Yup. That sweet taste underneath did have a hint of apple in it. It went surprisingly well with the coffee, though there were probably other flavors in there to lessen the coffee taste.

"Any more news about Bob Woodard?" he asked quietly, steering them toward the back of the inn. Past the gilded brass doors of the elevator was another set of broad doors that led to the inner courtyard of the inn.

"Not really," AJ said. She couldn't help but stiffen up.

"I see," Roland said, leading them outside.

The inn itself formed a U-shape around a set of immaculate gardens, filled with colorful flowers and well-trimmed shrubs. A beautiful fountain proudly filled the center of the area, with benches all around it. AJ gratefully collapsed onto one of the smooth wooden seats, with Roland at her side.

The fountain itself was made out of brass turtles, piled high on each other's back until the top one stood seven feet in the air. Green patina covered the metal sculpture, and brilliant blue tile filled the basin underneath. The lovely sound of splashing water filled the quiet courtyard, spouts from the turtle's mouths shooting the water out. Being near water, as well as hearing it, helped AJ relax even more.

Roland sat close enough that AJ could feel his warmth radiating out. He'd learned early on that since water was her thing, bringing her back her to the fountain helped her recover her equilibrium.

"I told you about the vision, right?" AJ said, sipping her coffee and leaning against him, relishing the heat he put out. Like most men, he was a furnace, which made him a great companion on chilly nights. "Well, now everyone is saying that he was poisoned."

"Like how it showed in your vision?" Roland said.

AJ shrugged. "Sort of. He was surrounded by sickly green mist, which read as poison to me."

"Is the Milltown Open competition still going on as planned?" Roland asked.

"It is," AJ said. "I don't think anyone wanted to cancel it for Bob Woodard's death."

Roland snorted. "And good riddance?" he said.

AJ opened her mouth then closed it again. She didn't

want to speak ill of the dead. However, Bob had gone out of his way to be a pain in the ass.

"Yeah, I figure the police aren't going to be wanting for suspects," she said. "He wasn't well liked."

"They already have one," Roland said. "They brought someone in this morning."

"Really? So soon?" AJ said.

She told herself that she should feel relief, that she wasn't going to be called on to solve yet another murder in her small town. However, she'd be lying to herself. Part of her wanted to help with this crime. There was a feeling of obligation there.

Not so that she could help out whoever had done this to Bob. No, really.

"Yeah, just a sec," Roland said, pulling out his phone and scrolling to the Milltown app. "Lili Jang? One of the competitors?"

"No," AJ said, pulling the phone over so she could see. Though there wasn't an official announcement of an arrest yet, Lili had been put into the back of a police car and taken to the station.

"I have to go," AJ said, abruptly standing.

"What, do you know her?" Roland said.

"Yeah, I told you about meeting her last night," AJ said. She could see that he was upset. He'd probably been wanting to take her out to lunch. "She was one of my developers, back when I worked at that tech startup in Seattle. She didn't do it. I'm certain of it. She wouldn't do that sort of thing," AJ continued as she started walking back toward the doors of the inn.

"Woah," Roland said, standing up and reaching out

one very warm hand, wrapping it around AJ's forearm. "When was the last time you saw her on a regular basis?"

"Over two years ago," AJ admitted. "But she hasn't changed that much. I honestly don't think she's changed at all. Meeting her yesterday, at the inn, well, I'd say she hasn't changed. Not enough to become a killer." AJ shuddered. Though Lili wasn't overly emotional, she hadn't grown cold and calloused. Had she?

"Why are you certain she wouldn't have done it?" Roland said.

"She's something of a germaphobe," AJ said. "She won't even shake people's hands, not if she doesn't have to. If she were going to kill somebody? Poison would be the last thing she'd use." AJ nodded firmly.

Not as if Lili didn't have the ability to kill someone. No, it was the method that was all wrong.

Roland smirked at her. "I see," he said. His phone suddenly buzzed angrily at him, some sort of urgent message. He glanced at his phone, then sighed. "I'm going to have to get going as well," he said. "But call me later. Tell me what's going on. I'm here to help."

"Thanks," AJ said, leaning over and giving his soft beard another kiss before hurrying through the doors into the inn.

It was nice to have that support. To have someone so solid and dependable in her corner. Even if he didn't know about all of her life.

At the same time, she had a sinking feeling that proving that Lili hadn't killed Bob Woodward was going to take all her magic, all her skill, as well as a tremendous amount of luck.

Hopefully, that would be enough.

Chapter Six

AJ told Sooli that she'd be back in a short time, then hurried out of the inn and down the street. Even though Milltown was tiny, a small ride-share company had started up, with two cars generally available, one on the north end of town and one on the south side. Fortunately, the car was there, ready for her to rent. She told herself yet again that at some point she was going to have to buy a car—but it had yet to be necessary, particularly with the rideshare vehicles.

The police station was at the far end of Milltown—a town that the locals jokingly said was two miles long and two blocks wide. While AJ regularly walked from one end of the town to the other, she didn't expect Lili to want to do that. If she was remembering correctly, Lili wasn't fond of anything that might make her sweat. Despite regularly working with fire. AJ would bet that in addition to fans inside her smokers, Lili also had fans blowing on her.

The police station hadn't changed at all since the last

time AJ had been there, three months before, after being kidnapped by the man who'd killed the other psychic in town. It still was short, squat, and mean-looking, with frosted windows reinforced with chicken wire and a solid gray door that was probably bomb proof. The interior doors were just as solid, and many security cameras peered down at her as she pulled the heavy doors open.

No one was standing on either side of the counter, but an elderly woman sat behind it, her gray hair a riot of curls. She smiled at AJ as she walked in.

Officer Toni, if AJ was remembering correctly.

Yes, there was the smell of burnt coffee in the air. Officer Brendan had warned her about that.

"Hi there, I'm here to pick up Lili Jang," AJ said as if that were the most natural thing in the world, as if perhaps the woman had called her.

"Okay?" Officer Toni said. "Just a second, I'll see if she'd ready to go."

AJ gave her a bright smile. "Thank you."

Again, she didn't like lying to the police, coming to pick up Lili before she'd been called or asked to, but in this case, it felt absolutely necessary.

"Officer Brendan wants to speak with you," Officer Toni said as she came back to the desk.

AJ kept her smile, but inside, she sighed.

Great. She really didn't want to get involved with the police. However, it appeared as though she didn't have a choice.

AJ was escorted into one of the side rooms, possibly the one she'd been in before. A skinny, oblong table made out of a pale wood took up most of the center of it, with chairs certain to cause backaches scattered around the edges.

"Can I get you some coffee?" Officer Toni asked before she left.

"No, thank you, I just had some," AJ was able to reply truthfully.

"It's a fresh pot," Officer Toni said, as if that should be an enticement.

"No, really, thank you," AJ said firmly. "I've had enough for the day."

Officer Toni gave her a tight-lipped smile, nodded, and left.

Did no one drink Officer Toni's coffee? Was that starting to make her feel bad? AJ didn't know, and she wasn't about to throw herself on that sword. She'd been spoiled by the great coffee from the Storm Brew Café, at least most of the time. Sometimes Juli, the regular barista, had a replacement, and what they brewed wasn't always as good.

AJ didn't have to wait long before Officer Brendan came in. He looked more grim than usual, his goofball smile missing, his gray eyes serious. His perfectly round head was meticulously shaved, and he looked older than he usually did.

AJ sighed.

"I'm not surprised to see you here," he said as he took a seat, gesturing for AJ to sit as well.

"Oh? Why is that?" AJ said.

"I'm assuming you have some intelligence about the recent death," Brendan said. Finally, a small smile played on his lips.

"I don't, actually," AJ said, putting as much regret as she could into the words. "I'm really here for Lili Jang. She's, well, she's not a friend. But she's a good person. A good acquaintance."

"Really?" Officer Brendan said, sounding surprised.

"She used to work for me, when I was in Seattle," AJ explained. "We were both part of the same tech startup."

Officer Brendan nodded. "Okay," he said. "What else can you tell me about her?"

"I haven't seen her today. But I'd bet she'd wearing a peach colored T-shirt and black jeans," AJ said. "She always wears the same clothes. It's one less decision she has to make in the mornings."

Officer Brendan looked impressed by that, his eyes widening. "What else can you tell me?"

"She's something of a germaphobe," AJ continued. "She wouldn't use poison. Wouldn't touch it."

Officer Brendan grimaced at that, but didn't comment. "When was the last time you saw her?"

"Yesterday afternoon, at the inn. I'm not sure if she'd just checked in or not," AJ said. She didn't recall seeing any luggage with Lili. "She told me that she'd retired from doing computer programming about a year ago and was dedicating her time to being on the BBQ competition circuit."

Officer Brendan nodded at that. "Yeah, she's got something of a reputation with her competitors."

"She didn't do it," AJ said firmly. "She didn't kill Bob Woodard."

"Are you sure?" Officer Brendan asked, giving her a sly grin.

AJ could tell that Officer Brendan would really like for AJ to admit that she'd had a vision or something, to give him the satisfaction that she knew something more about this case.

"I'm as certain as I can be," AJ said. "She's a good person. She wouldn't do this."

The grimace Officer Brendan gave her in response didn't do much to allay her fears.

After considering her for a few moments, Officer Brendan gave her a nod. "We're just about done questioning her. She's still a person of interest. But we haven't arrested her, and she is free to go."

"Thank you," AJ said, more relieved than she could express.

"And do let me know if you have any other information about this case," Officer Brendan said. "Whether officially or unofficially."

AJ smiled at him. He was honestly trying to do the best he could. She was glad she got to see him and not his partner, Officer Naomi, who was much more of a hard ass.

"I will," AJ said, though she knew she might be lying to the police once again. She couldn't guarantee that if something psychic happened that she'd come talk to them. But she might.

AJ waited out in the front office as police officers came and went. It took another forty minutes before Lili Jang was escorted forward.

"Do not leave town," Lili was warned by Officer Naomi.

"I understand," Lili said. She looked wan, her skin pale under its naturally dark color.

AJ knew that if Lili was on the BBQ circuit, she would have a few days between contests before she had to be at the next one. Hopefully the next contest was close enough to drive to in a day or so, and she wouldn't have to do something stupid like drive all the way across country in three days.

Lili didn't say anything more as AJ led the way out of the station, silently walking to AJ's rental. It wasn't until after AJ had started the car that Lili said anything.

"Thank you for coming to get me," she said softly.

AJ nodded. "Am I taking you back to the camping grounds? Or to the hotel?" The hotel was north of the police station, while the campground was south.

Lili grimaced. "The hotel. I want a real shower."

"All right," AJ said. After a few moments, she finally had to ask, "What happened?"

"I don't know!" Lili said. Though she spoke in her usual monotone, even AJ could tell the other woman was angry. "The group that I generally hang out with at competitions invited me to come and have a meal with them. It was a pot luck. I made steamed buns, filled with smoked pork."

"That sounds good," AJ said.

"They were amazing," Lili assured her. "But...somehow, my dish got ruined."

"Ruined? How?" AJ asked, surprised. Lili hadn't done something like burn the food, had she? Unless something had gone wrong with one of her timers, Lili was likely to be very precise with her temperatures.

"Someone knocked the tray over, off the table, before anyone could have any," Lili complained. "Anyone except Bob Woodard."

AJ nodded, seeing the problem immediately. If Bob had been the only one to have one of the dishes at a potluck, that did make Lili's contribution more suspicious.

"Did you poison him?"

"Of course not," Lili said. "If I was going to kill someone, I wouldn't use poison. Too messy. Too unpredictable. Even if you got the person's weight right, you never know about their metabolism."

AJ nodded. That was what she assumed.

Then she had a strange thought.

"You didn't, perchance, tell the police that, did you?" AJ asked.

"I told them," Lili said.

"Exactly like that?"

"Uhmm, yeah?"

AJ just shook her head. She could only imagine how well that went over. Possibly it had been one of the reasons why they'd brought Lili in for questioning in the first place.

"Seriously. If I were going to kill someone, I'd make sure we were private. Knock them out with three times the amount of whatever sedative I could whip up, dismember the body, and take it to a local pig farm," Lili continued. "Or I'd have the chemicals necessary to dissolve the bones. Pigs sometimes don't eat everything. Plus coffee grounds."

"Why coffee grounds?" AJ asked, assuming she was going to regret learning the answer.

"Messes up most of the forensics tests that they do these days, at least according to the *Real True Crime* show I've been watching. Dousing a body in coffee grounds hides a lot of evidence," Lili said, sounding as serious as always.

AJ sighed. "Okay, first of all, you really can't go around telling people that sort of thing. Especially the police. It'll just make them suspicious."

"But I didn't do it," Lili said.

"I know that," AJ said. And despite Lili's interest in these grotesque topics, she still firmly believed that. "Other people don't. And they're already suspicious of you."

"Fine," Lili said, obviously frustrated.

"Did you have a history with Bob Woodard?" AJ said.

It was Lili's turn to shrug. "We had sex once. It wasn't very good."

"You what?" AJ had to ask.

She wasn't shouting. Really.

"It was...six months ago?" Lili said. "He approached me. I had tried sex once before, many years ago, back in college. Figured I should try it again, see if I liked it better this time. I didn't."

AJ was glad that they were paused at a stoplight so her brain could reset itself. She'd known that Lili was a bit different than other people. This was just further confirmation.

"Did you tell the police this as well?"

"They already seemed to know that we had been

together." Lili paused, squinching up her nose as she thought. "I believe they accused us of being an item? Like something on a menu? I'm not sure."

So...obviously someone had set Lili up, for the police to already know that.

Someone in the BBQ community she hung out with. Lili wouldn't have lied about what she'd done with Bob. Wouldn't have necessarily understood that she wasn't supposed to talk about such things.

Or how she'd felt about having an encounter with Bob afterward.

"Okay, so someone set you up," AJ said. "Are there any people among your BBQ competitors who don't like you?"

"Maybe?" Lili guessed. "It's difficult for me to tell who is just awkward around me and who would have feelings."

AJ nodded. That made sense.

"You know I didn't do it, right?" Lili said, suddenly needing reassurance.

"I do," AJ said.

No, someone else had set Lili up.

And AJ was going to have to find them.

Chapter Seven

AJ spent the rest of Friday afternoon working at the inn, helping out the front desk during the rush of weekend check-in, slipping away to her office to finish paperwork when she could.

Once AJ was finally finished with work, she walked down Main Street, dodging tourists, before she turned and walked up one of the side streets. Much of Milltown was built onto the side of a hill, overlooking the ocean.

Her sister Bea had a vacation cottage in one of the neighborhoods built up off the main drag. Every time AJ had to walk up that hill she was reminded of why she lived where she did, where it was a relatively short, and easy, walk to the inn.

Instead of this massive hill that made her calves ache every time she huffed her way up it.

AJ didn't consider herself an athlete. She did go swimming in the ocean regularly, and since coming here to Milltown, she'd joined a group doing yoga at the community center most every Sunday. However, if she were intent on doing some serious conditioning, all she'd have to do was run up and down this hill a few times a day.

Bea's vacation house stood at the end of a quiet cul-de-sac. She'd just moved down for the summer. And though Bea's stood out, there were a few others that could also (generously) be called eclectic: like the house with all the carvings out front, including a full-sized deer whose antlers formed a heart; the yard with the garden that was so overgrown it nearly hid the house; as well as the place that had, at current count, fourteen different bird feeders either standing in the yard or hanging from the eves, and those were only the ones that AJ could see— no idea how many more were in the backyard.

In some ways, Bea's house was very similar to its neighbors—a one-story rambler with broad windows on either side of the center doorway, a gray-shingled roof, and a garage attached to the south side.

The colors, however...

Her sister Bea was a painter. AJ would bet that whenever Bea had left-over paint, she came outside and just threw it randomly against the walls. There was no pattern, no discernable figures. Just an explosion of color.

An unfamiliar car sat in the driveway. Had Peter, Bea's husband, decided to come and visit unexpectedly? Or was this a client come to pick up a painting?

AJ let herself into the house without knocking. She had her own key, just as Bea had a key to AJ's house. Plus, if Bea was busy painting, she wouldn't answer the door anyway.

AJ called out as she came in, "Hello! Anyone home?"

"Back here!" Bea replied.

AJ took off her shoes and made her way toward the sunken living room that took up much of the left side of the front of the house, with the kitchen behind it. The master bedroom and bath were to the right, and a guest room and bath were to the left.

AJ came to a full stop when she saw who was sitting on the couch beside Bea.

"Hello, dear," came the familiar alto.

"Uhm, hi, Mom," AJ finally found herself able to say. "What are you doing here?" she said, shooting a glare at Bea, to see if her sister had known about their mother coming down and just hadn't said anything about it.

From the guilty look on Bea's face, it appeared that she'd at least had some foreknowledge.

Of course, if AJ said anything, Bea would just tease her about what a bad psychic she was.

For the brief moment they stayed frozen, AJ was able to look at her mom and make comparisons. Her hair was dark, like AJ's, though it did have a few strands of white going through it—probably artfully placed, not natural. While Mom shared the same thinner build that AJ had, she had Bea's beautiful blue eyes and pert nose. She was also shorter than AJ, more like Bea.

Even just sitting there, Irene Steward struck AJ as vibrant and full of a harsh energy, ready to either sweep you along in her wake or cut you down. She looked a little older than the last time AJ had seen her—which, honestly, was probably over a year ago—with more wrinkles around the corners of her eyes, and certainly more age spots on her hands. However, all in all, she looked healthy, bright, and probably scheming.

"Is everything all right?" AJ asked as she came over for the air kisses that her mom bestowed on her.

While AJ and Bea had started hugging, AJ didn't expect the rest of her family to ever become tactile.

"Yes, yes, everything's fine," Mom replied, sounding exacerbated. "Why does everyone keep asking that?"

"Because you've never been here before," Bea pointed out, "no matter how many times I've invited you down."

"It's a long drive down here from Seattle, and I've always been busy," Mom said, dismissing Bea's complaint as if it weren't important in the least. "Besides, how could I say no to your latest temptation? BBQ *and* a possible love interest of your sister's?"

"You told her?" AJ fumed at Bea. She didn't have to add, *You are so dead.* Bea's gulp and slight paling of her face told AJ that her sister had heard the words loud and clear.

"Please," Mom said, stepping in as she always did. "She didn't have to. It was obvious that something must be keeping you...here."

AJ closed her eyes rather than roll them at that statement. She might have hurt something if she had.

"I like it here, Mom," AJ said. As she'd told her mom more than once during their infrequent calls. Probably the last time she'd talked with her mom had been five months before, speaking to her over the holidays. "I have my own business. I do good work."

"As a psychic?" Mom said, sounding as bewildered as AJ occasionally felt when reviewing her life, looking back at where she'd been and comparing it to where she was now.

"Yes, Mom," AJ said. "A successful one."

Mom waved that away. "Of course you're successful. I wouldn't expect you to be anything but."

"So are you here for the weekend?" AJ said, trying to be polite and not snap at her mom.

"At least," Mom said. "You're going to be busy all weekend, so I actually wasn't planning on leaving until sometime next week."

Bea nodded. "Of course! You can stay as long as you want."

AJ forced a smile. It was the polite thing for Bea to say. She probably would have said the same thing if Mom had shown up on her doorstep.

But really, AJ wasn't certain she believed her mother, the reasons why she was down here, or how long she'd stay.

No, something else was going on.

And AJ wasn't sure she wanted to find out what.

Chapter Eight

Dinner went as well as could be imagined. AJ and Bea carried much of the conversational weight, bringing their mother up to speed on the town and most of the various things happening there. It turned out that Bea had only had a few hours' warning of their mother's impending visit—she'd called at the start of the drive down—not days' or weeks' worth. So her sister had been able to supplement the dinner that she'd prepared, making enough for the three of them.

It *was* good to listen to Mom talk about the charities she supported, the behind-the-scenes fighting that went on. Mom was a powerhouse, as always.

Still, something felt a little off. There was a hesitancy that AJ wasn't used to seeing in her mom, as if she was being more careful with her words than usual. She asked her mom about her health a couple of times, just to have the questions waved off.

AJ even dared ask about their father, the man who'd abandoned them early in life. They'd never wanted for anything material—their father had always thrown money at them. But once they'd turned into teenagers, he'd disappeared out of their lives, replying monosyllabically to any texts, getting off the phone within minutes of them calling for birthdays or other holidays. AJ and then Bea had stopped trying to contact him before they'd turned eighteen.

"Why would you ask about him?" Mom said, very confused. "I haven't had any more contact with him than you have. Unless he's called?"

AJ glanced over at Bea, who just shook her head.

Nope. Their long-absent father wasn't why their mom was there now.

"So, tell me about this psychic business," Mom finally asked after they'd finished not only the heavenly pot roast and grilled veggies, but the amazing apple pie that Bea had bought. They were all back in the living room sitting on the couch, each holding a full glass of a sweetish merlot. Since AJ was walking home, she wasn't worried about drinking too much, even if, with menopause, she'd really turned into a lightweight.

AJ's eyes flicked over to Bea, sitting on the far side of Mom. She wasn't sure how much to tell her mom. Bea knew, well, everything, not just about AJ's visions but her magic as well.

Bea shrugged, obviously having no idea either.

AJ rolled her eyes. *SO* not helping.

"What do you want to know?" AJ asked. "I run the business out of my house."

Mom nodded. "I'd like to see your place, sometime."

AJ nodded, a little surprised. Her mom had come to

her house in Seattle once, for the house-warming party. Had viciously complained about the lack of parking, and so had made a point of never going back, always insisting that AJ meet her someplace more convenient.

"You're welcome to stop by the house any time," AJ said. "It's an old Victorian, down on the beach. It needed some work before I could move in, but it's all fixed up now." Like upgrading the foundation, completely redoing the kitchen and bathroom on the first floor, creating her reading room, new paint, and so on. The second floor hadn't needed as much work, mainly just paint and some sprucing up.

"She wouldn't follow my ideas for a color scheme for the outside of the house," Bea said pouting.

"That's because it was already like living in an ice cream parlor. Your colors wouldn't have made it any better," AJ pointed out.

Bea rolled her eyes and shook her head, grinning.

"Anyway, I have a reading room in the front, where I do all my tarot card readings," AJ continued.

She didn't add that she also kept her scrying bowl there, not certain if she wanted to tell her mom about the visions she had.

And she certainly wasn't going to mention the ability to do magic, or transform water.

"Did you know that your great aunt read tarot cards?" Mom asked, musing. "Quite the scandal, back in the day."

"No, really?" AJ asked, curious. She had no idea that any of her maternal relatives had been anything other than exactly what they were supposed to be, doing exactly what they'd been told to do.

Mom nodded, taking a sip of wine. "I was only a teenager. But I remember my parents talking about it. My grandmother's sister. Great Aunt Loraine. They also said she was an alcoholic. I only remember meeting her a few times. She taught me to play poker, much to my parents' chagrin."

"Huh," was all that AJ could say. She knew that magic often ran in families. Gabby had some sort of issue with her bio-dad, and so didn't know that side of her family at all, but had assumed that her magic had come from there, as her mom's side were generally, according to her, "distressingly normal."

"Plus, I seem to recall you doing things as a teenager," Mom continued. "Like answering the phone before it rang."

"You knew about that?" AJ asked, surprised. She remembered trying so hard to fit in, to not let her mom know that she was different. While Bea had gone the opposite direction, and had become as artistic and outspoken as she could be.

AJ had rebelled in other ways, such as going into the computer business instead of finance, as her mom had wanted her to. However, dealing with numbers day in and day out made AJ crazy.

Crazier.

Whatever.

Mom gave her what amounted to a possessive smile. "I did," she purred. "I pretended I didn't, of course. I let you have your illusions."

"Gee, thanks," AJ said dryly. Maybe, perhaps, if her mom had said something, AJ wouldn't have felt so bad, so odd about it. Might not have denied and hidden whatever talent she'd had for so many years.

Then again, Gabby had told her that frequently, a woman didn't come into her power until she'd reached menopause, those hot flashes transforming into power surges.

"Will you do a reading for me? Before I leave?" Mom asked, gazing at her curiously.

AJ opened her mouth and then shut it again. "I will," she said. "Happy to," she added after a moment, realizing that she actually *was* happy to do a reading for her mother.

It would kind of be like the other readings that she did, when she didn't know the person very well or the question that they wanted answered. Honestly, how much did she know about her own mother? Beyond the public face that she showed? It wasn't that her mom was ultra-private about things. Rather, it was more like AJ wasn't sure how much more there was to see beyond what her mom presented to the outside world.

Maybe there was a lot more there.

Or perhaps, there wasn't.

Bea had to brag about AJ working with the police to solve a couple of crimes that had occurred in Milltown. Which led to them talking about the poisoning that had just happened at the BBQ competition.

AJ was able to fill them in on the details—the potluck, and Bob being the only one sick.

"What, do you know the person the police brought in

for questioning?" Bea asked. Then she snorted and shook her head. "Of course you do."

"Hey, that's my line!" AJ complained. Really, Bea knew *everyone* in Milltown. Anytime they went out to eat, or even just picked up coffee, they were still stopped half a dozen times by people who wanted to say hello or to talk with Bea.

"She was one of my developers, from the last company I worked at," AJ explained.

"Did she do it?" Bea asked expectantly.

"No," AJ said. "Someone set her up."

"Oh!" Bea exclaimed. "And you're going to help the police figure out who the real killer is, right?"

"Something like that," AJ said, downplaying her role, particularly in front of their mom.

"I'm not sure I like you getting involved in a murder this way," Mom said, giving AJ a hard look.

AJ shrugged. "Would you rather that an innocent person went to jail?"

"No," her mother said, narrowing her eyes. "But you don't have any experience at this. Leave this to the professionals."

Bea snorted. "As if."

AJ bit her lips together. Mom was right, in a way. It really was an issue for the police to handle.

On the other hand, she was certain that Lili had been set up. And also, that she should get involved. She was the one who'd had a vision involving the dead man.

"I never knew you had such an altruistic streak in you," Mom commented after a few moments. "Then again, I suppose it's like my charity work."

AJ pressed her lips together so she wouldn't snap at her mom.

No, it was *nothing* like her mother's charity work. Her mom did charity work for the power, in order to see and be seen, not because there were any causes that her mom actually believed in.

So AJ let the comment slide, Bea changed the topic, and the three of them managed to spend the rest of the evening comfortably chatting, without anyone blowing up at each other.

AJ would count that as a win.

Chapter Nine

Normally, AJ had Saturdays off from the inn, and instead, just saw clients. This weekend, though, was the BBQ competition, the inn was one of the major sponsors of the event, and she was on the town council committee. There weren't any emergency meetings that morning but she still got up early and headed down to Sandy Point to see if there was anything that needed doing.

If the tide had been in, AJ would have had to walk down Main Street, from one end of the town to the other. However, the tide was out—far out, the water just a gray streak past the golden sand—so she walked along the beach instead. It was still beautiful, with a clear blue sky, strands of clouds strung out across it, and the wind not too bad. The sun wasn't warm, not yet, but AJ predicted that if the day stayed clear, it would be close to summertime temperatures by midafternoon.

AJ walked down toward the water's edge, where the sand was more compact. Terns and other long-legged birds raced beside her. Strands of seaweed lay strung like banners along the shore, showing where the waves had been. The raucous call of seagulls cut through the air, hurling their defiance to all.

AJ loved being this close to the ocean. Water was her element. Maybe tomorrow she'd get up early and take a swim. Sure, Roland called her crazy for being in the ocean this time of year, even with a wetsuit.

However, the cold didn't bother AJ that much. Not when it was cold water. Cold anything else, yeah, since menopause she'd really grown sensitive to it.

Sandy Point was just what it sounded like—a large "point" of land that jutted out into the ocean, forming a small bay to the south of it. Sandy's Grill was set inland just a bit from the edge, on more solid ground. Sandy herself had been the driving force behind the BBQ competition, and been the initial contact between Mill-town and the LCBA.

AJ had wondered if Sandy was the woman's real name, or if everyone just called her that, as Sandy Point and Sandy's Grill had both existed long before Sandy, the latest owner, had come into town and bought the place.

Normally, Sandy's Grill was only open for lunch and dinner. That morning, though, there was a long line at the take-away window, people carrying bags of donuts and pastries as they left, as well as steaming cups of coffee. In addition, one of the ubiquitous food trucks from the area had set up shop in the parking lot, selling breakfast tacos and burritos.

Were all these people here for the competition? She'd think that those in the campground would be making their own breakfast. Or maybe these were the judges or others affiliated with the LCBA.

AJ braved the line at Sandy's, as she'd already had breakfast. Though the burritos did smell awfully good, she didn't need more food. The air was just crisp enough that more coffee—or anything warm, quite frankly—sounded astounding.

"Are you here for the competition?" AJ asked the people behind her, as she didn't recognize them.

"Yes!" gushed the older woman with a merry grin. She had faded hazel eyes and white hair, but also big dimples when she smiled.

"It's her religion," the man commented.

"Oh, shush, you," the woman commanded mock-sternly. "We're so thrilled to have a competition occurring so close to where we live! Otherwise, we have to go camp to follow our teams."

AJ nodded politely, while the man looked on with fondness.

Yup. New religion, for certain.

"I'm AJ Steward," she said, introducing herself. "I work here, at the Bridgewater Inn. We're one of the sponsors of the contest."

"Ohhh!" the woman exclaimed. "Those hot springs you have in back are marvelous!" She introduced herself as Rose, with her husband Doug, and they chatted amicably as they waited for their turn at the takeout window.

Rose did indeed know quite a bit about the various teams of competitors. Her husband teased her about her spreadsheet, and how she kept track of wins and losses.

"I have a good feeling about Las Chicas this time," Rose said with a nod. "They don't always win—it's like they get distracted from the competition sometimes, and don't turn in their meat when they should. But hopefully, this time, they'll take the grand championship."

AJ thought for a moment, then had to ask, "Okay, I'm pretty sure someone explained to me what the championship was at one point. But pre-coffee, I've completely forgotten."

"Oh! Let me explain. The four proteins this competition is showcasing are brisket, pulled pork, ribs, and chicken. Most competitions have all four, but some competitions will just do one or two, along with a specialty item, such as ribeye or tri-tip," Rose said.

She smiled up at her husband. "I still remember that amazing ribeye we had last year."

"There were quite a few good ones at that competition," her husband agreed.

"At the end of the competition, that is, tomorrow afternoon, they'll announce the top ten winners in all the categories. They'll only hand out prizes, that is, 'give the call' for the top five, though," Rose said.

AJ nodded. This sounded vaguely familiar.

"Then, the LBCA will tally all the results for every team, and hand out the runner up, champion, and grand championship awards to the teams that scored best overall, in all four categories. Sometimes it's an upset, with a team not getting a call in all the categories, but still coming out on top," Rose concluded.

"Are you two judges?" AJ asked.

Rose gave her a wry grin. "I've taken the class, and

learned all about the judging. But the problem is, I'm allergic to nightshades. And everyone uses some sort of pepper or paprika in their rubs. The pain just isn't worth getting to try all those meats." She still sounded wistful.

"It's enough to come to the competitions and try what we can," Doug told his wife, patting her shoulder.

"I know," Rose said. "And we've thought about joining one, in the backyard category. But the taste profile of my product is just going to be so very different from what the judges are used to."

"Backyard category?" AJ asked as the line inched forward.

"Some competitions are divided into professional teams and those who do backyard BBQ," Doug explained. "I keep telling her that we'd sweep the latter. Her brisket is that good. As is her pulled pork."

Rose grimaced. "I still need to work on my ribs. And I don't think I'll ever come up to competition standard with my chicken. It's just too hard to cook to competition standards."

"I will certainly keep in mind that perhaps next year, we expand the competition to include a backyard category," AJ promised them as she finally, *finally* reached the window.

"Thank you!" Rose said.

Doug caught her eye in a meaningful fashion and nodded. AJ realized that he was letting her know that his thanks would be double that of his wife's if she could get the opportunity to compete.

AJ waved goodbye to the couple and started across

the parking lot with her coffee, heading toward the competition area.

Just past Sandy's Grill and the adjacent parking lot stood a large, flat park, at least the size of a football field. Normally, the area wasn't blocked off, but for the competition, large, white plastic barrels filled with sand had been rolled into place, with ropes strung between them. They wouldn't keep out anyone intent on gaining entrance. However, in order to taste any of the available BBQ, you had to go through the front gate and buy tokens.

In addition to the barrels, trucks and tents now encircled the area. Not all the competitors would be selling samples of their product, but there were enough to make a good show. At the far eastern end, a small stage had been set up and live music would be playing all day, starting at noon.

To the north stood one big, long white tent. That was where the contestants would turn in their meats at various times during the day. The judges would be sequestered in the tent all afternoon tomorrow.

The smell of woodsmoke and cooked meats filled the air. AJ debated for a few moments going back to the breakfast burrito truck, but decided that it would be better if she was a little hungry going into lunchtime, particularly since she was not only meeting Bea but their mom as well.

AJ walked toward the tent, showing her credentials to the two older women sipping coffee at the entrance. They nodded her in, and AJ went to check that everything was okay.

Sandy stood in the middle of the open judging area, as well as Fred Hansen, Lionel Jackson, and Caitlin Lee. Long tables were piled on one side, as well as chairs.

Nothing had been set up yet? Was this a problem?

"Sure, we could start setting up," Sandy was explaining, waving at the stack of tables in the corner. She wore her usual crabbing boots over a set of hard-used denim overalls. Her jacket had probably been white at one point. Or maybe it had always been that particular shade of off-white. It hadn't always had those stains on it.

AJ was surprised that Sandy wasn't looking more polished. Maybe she hadn't expected to have to do anything official that morning.

"However, *I* think we should wait until we have the final count of contestants before we know how many judges we need," Sandy continued.

"Well, we know we need at least thirty-seven chairs," Lionel said, obviously trying to sound reasonable. "There's a requirement of at least one judge per team." Lionel looked cool and suave, as always, much hipper than the rest of them, in his beige tweed jacket that had red threads running through it, with a complementary red scarf. His black skin looked amazing against the off-white turtleneck. He could have stepped from the pages of a fashion magazine.

"Are contestants likely to back out at the last minute?" Caitlin asked. She, on the other hand, looked downright frumpy that morning, in contrast to her usual office-chic apparel. That midthigh coat of hers was too tight, her black leggings were faded, and the denim shirt was three sizes too big. Her short brown hair looked as though it had been flooffed by someone running their fingers through product that had been left in it overnight.

"It isn't always the call of the contestants," Sandy said, grimacing. "The meat inspections are going to start in a bit. Not everyone who signed up for our inaugural contest are professionals. If their meat hasn't been stored properly and isn't at the correct temperature, they'll be disqualified."

"So we have backyard BBQ teams then, this year, people who aren't used to this sort of competition," AJ said.

"Technically, no," Sandy said. "We don't have a category for backyard, at least not this year. However, about a quarter of the teams are newly formed."

"I still think we should get the chairs and tables set up now," Lionel said. "Sure, we'll probably have to clean them up again, before tomorrow's judging. But better to be set up now, and look professional about it."

"What do you think, AJ?" Fred asked. Fred looked as he normally did, in a flannel shirt, jeans, and work boots that copied Roland's style. However, AJ would bet that Fred had never done a day of hard physical labor in his entire life. He always found other people to do the work for him.

In fact, the only thing he worked on these days were his mystery novels, loudly proclaiming AJ as his muse.

Fred's hairline was still receding. AJ wondered at what point he'd give up the fight and just start shaving his entire head, removing the little wisps that clung to the edges of it. His chin jutted out, as if to balance his face.

His gray eyes were kind, and frequently sparkled with mischief.

"It doesn't take long to set up tables and chairs," AJ said. "With all of us, it might take five minutes. Tops. Cleaning them afterward, because yes, people will sneak in here to use them, won't take too much time tomorrow morning, either. Besides, since we're serving food, don't they have to be inspected as well?"

Fred sighed at her, obviously disappointed in her answer.

She wasn't sure where Fred's aversion to work had originated. It was certainly one of his primary themes now.

"Then let's get it done, people," Sandy proclaimed, stalking over to the stack of folded up tables and lifting the top one off herself.

Not to be outdone, Caitlin also walked over to grab one herself. However, Lionel grabbed the other end and helped her lift it, so they could work together.

Fred grimaced, but then nodded at AJ and said, "Shall we?"

"Sure," AJ said. They picked up the next table and set it in line with the ones that the others had already unfolded.

"So, what do you know about the latest murder?" Fred asked, trying to sound casual but failing miserably.

As Fred was widely known as the town gossip, he generally knew more than most people about any of the happenings in Milltown. Even if his writing had taken him away from being at the center of things, a fact he frequently complained about.

"The woman the police picked up? Lili Jang?" AJ said, making sure that she had Fred's full attention. "She didn't do it."

"Really?" Fred said eagerly. He looked around, but the others had all moved back to the far corner to pick up more tables. "You *know* know this?"

AJ wasn't exactly certain what Fred was asking, though she suspected that he was trying to obliquely ask her if she'd had a vision about it.

"I used to work with her in Seattle. She's being set up," AJ said firmly.

"Ohhh," Fred said. "A personal angle. I like that. I might have to use that in the next novel."

AJ rolled her eyes. "Come on," she said, walking back to the tables to get another one.

"How is she being set up?" Fred asked.

AJ explained what she knew, about how Lili had had a one-night stand with Bob Woodard, how Bob was the only one who'd tried her food at the potluck.

"So we're looking for someone who has a relationship with Lili, as well as with Bob," Fred said. "Probably not one of the newer teams then, but a professional."

"Good thinking," AJ said, nodding. That at least eliminated about a quarter of the thirty-seven teams, as they were newly formed and probably didn't know either Lili or Bob.

"Anything else you'd recommend? Since you're the professional mystery solver?" AJ teased. Fred still hadn't published his first novel, though it was all ready. He'd decided to work with a small independent publisher, whom he would pay upfront to help him publish. He'd chosen a day in the week before Halloween for the first one to come out.

Fred thought seriously for a moment. "The poison hasn't been identified," he said slowly. "But I may have heard a rumor that poor Bob's lips as well as his fingertips turned blue from it."

"Couldn't that be caused by a lack of oxygen?" AJ asked.

"Possibly, but I'd heard that the color was unnatural."

"Hmmm," AJ said. She was silent as they walked back across the space and got the last of the tables, as Sandy and the others appeared to have had some sort of competition going, to see who could set up the most tables the quickest.

"Who in town would know about poisons?" AJ asked after a bit.

"I'd start with Naimh Fogarty," Fred said. "She runs Scents by the Sea. In addition to candles, she also sells teas. She knows more herbal lore than anyone else in town."

AJ thought for a moment. "Neev?" she asked.

Fred grinned at her. "She spells her name the traditional Irish way, N-A-I-M-H. But it's pronounced *neev*."

"Oh!" AJ said. Yes, she remembered meeting Naimh at a chamber of commerce meeting, seeing that on the nametag of a tall, buxom woman with blue eyes and red hair that was fading to a beautiful shade of gold. However, AJ had never had the opportunity to go and ask Naimh how to pronounce her name. "I'll talk with her later this afternoon."

Thus resolved, AJ soon said goodbye and headed out.

She intended to stop by the campgrounds and check on Lili and Gabby, before meeting with her mother and Bea to have some lunch and BBQ.

As she stepped outside, she paused, taking in another deep breath of the crisp air.

At least it was nice out, though she wasn't certain how nice the rest of her day would be.

Chapter Ten

The campground, where most of the contestants were staying, was just across from the park, on the other side of Highway 101. In this part of its coastal stretch, 101 had just a single lane of traffic going either direction with a turn lane in the center.

AJ crossed the highway at a nearby light, then continued into the campground itself, heading straight for Gabby's camp. She didn't know where Lili was, but hopefully Gabby would know.

Las Chicas de Carne had a proud banner proclaiming their space, decorated with painted hunks of steak and ribs, hung in front of the massive RV parked there. Gabby and her sister Cecilia were sitting outside the camper at the picnic table, going over some notes. AJ assumed that Gabby's girlfriend, Elanor, was inside.

"Hey, AJ!" Gabby said, calling her over.

"Good morning," AJ said.

Like AJ and her sister, Gabby and Cecilia bore very little resemblance to each other. While Gabby was the shorter one, more heavyset with lots of curves, Cecilia was taller and thinner.

And starkly beautiful.

Gabby teased her sister about being the "face" of the group. She had modelesque good looks, perfectly symmetrical, with an oval face, enviable smooth skin and a smoldering smile. Roland, who'd met them as well when they'd all gone out to dinner, had made the comment that Cecilia had permanent bedroom eyes, dark and sultry, while Gabby's smile was pure joy.

While both Gabby and Cecilia had the dark skin of their Hispanic heritage, Elanor proclaimed herself the white girl of the group. She had what AJ would refer to as peaches and cream skin, pure white and pink, with dirty-blonde hair and bright blue eyes. She'd originally come from England, arriving in the US to study at Berkeley Law. She was something of a disgrace to her family, having thrown aside the corporate world and fallen into something she loved so much more, namely, cooking.

Gabby was the fire mistress of the group, maintaining the fires in their offset smoker (Inez by name), Cecilia dealt with customers and was "front of house," whereas Elanor was the one who came up with the recipes for everything they served, including their own line of meat rubs and sauces.

"How is everyone doing this morning?" AJ asked, looking at the two sisters.

"Fine," Cecilia said, nodding tersely.

She didn't sound fine. Gabby didn't look happy, either.

"What's up?" AJ said as she sat down, lowering her

voice so that they wouldn't be sharing their business with everyone in the campsite.

"Little Miss Gabby here wants to experiment with some of our cook times," Cecilia complained. "Now is *not* the time to be trying new things. We need to use what works."

"But we've never cooked here before, so close to the ocean. The winds here are going to cool off Inez. We will need longer cook times if we want our product to be cooked all the way through," Gabby pointed out.

Cecilia sighed and shook her head. "We've been over this. The winds are mainly on the coast, not this far inland. We're blocked by the dunes over there and the park. And we have cooked in this sort of climate before. I don't know what's gotten into you!"

Gabby grimaced. "I don't know either. I just...feel that we need to start sooner than usual."

"But we can't start until after the meat inspection, right?" Cecilia pointed out. "So there's no point in moving around any of my timelines until after that occurs."

"Fine, you're right," Gabby said, sounding frustrated. "And that won't be until after one PM, right?" she said, looking first at Cecilia and then at AJ.

AJ shrugged. While she'd been told the timing of events for the competition, she hadn't bothered to keep good notes about everything. Sandy was responsible for many of those details.

"Yeah, I think you're right," Cecilia said. She turned and put on a pleasant smile for AJ. "How is your morning going? Hopefully your sister isn't giving you as hard of a time as mine is giving me."

AJ grinned at her. "Haven't talked with her yet. Then again, she has her hands full. My mother decided to come down for a surprise visit."

"That isn't a good thing?" Gabby guessed.

AJ sighed, feeling frustrated again. "She's never been down to visit Milltown before, even though Bea's had her vacation cottage down here for at least twenty years. I get the feeling that something else is up, but I don't know what."

"Maybe you should practice your farsense on that," Gabby said immediately. "See if you can figure out what's happening with her."

AJ nodded slowly. That made sense. However, she was loath to try to spy on her mother. Mom would tell her eventually what was going on.

"In the meanwhile, I figured I'd go and check on Lili, see how she's holding up this morning," AJ said. "But I don't know where her camp is."

"I'll walk you there," Gabby volunteered, hopping up from the table. "Since it appears that I'm *not* going to start cooking anytime soon."

Cecelia rolled her eyes but didn't otherwise comment.

AJ and Gabby walked down the paved road between the parked RVs and tents, enjoying the sunshine and all the trees. "This is a nicer campgrounds than a lot of the ones we stay at," Gabby commented after a few moments as they rounded the bend. "Sometimes we're parked right next to our neighbors, the RVs not three feet apart."

"That can't be fun," AJ said.

"You get used to it," Gabby said, shrugging. "Though we also tend to go to those competitions only once, or we find other places to camp."

"You looking forward to the competition?" AJ asked. "You seem...tense."

Gabby grimaced. "I don't honestly know if it's nerves that are getting to me or if there's something magical going on."

"Sharing the campground with a known killer can't be pleasant either," AJ pointed out.

Gabby nodded. "I know, right? I keep looking at people sideways, wondering if they were the person to poison Bob and to set Lili up to take the fall."

They walked around the bend. Just ahead, a large number of people were standing along the edge of the road, staring at the person behind the picnic table next to a tent. Angry words were being tossed into the camp asking what the person was doing and why she was still there.

AJ glanced at Gabby, who had a firm expression of annoyance set on her face.

"What's going on here?" Gabby shouted as they came walking up.

Some of the people started at the loud words, while others barely bothered glancing at Gabby.

"It isn't right that she's still here," said one heavy-set man. He was wearing a stained blue T-shirt that had sadly seen better days, stained black pants, and sneakers with holes in them. He had faded red hair and pale white skin. Freckles were scattered all over his face.

Gabby took a second look at him. "Wait, aren't you Rusty Thomas?" she asked, seeming surprised to see him.

"I am!" the man said, proud that someone had recognized him.

"I would think you'd be celebrating the fact that Bob Woodward is dead, not hassling an innocent woman," Gabby said pointedly.

Obviously, there was some background there that AJ wasn't privy to.

"Naw, Bob and I made up," Rusty assured her. "It was all just for the show, you know?"

A man who'd come walking up at the same time they had snorted loudly. "That's not what y'all's Birdy account says," he proclaimed loudly in a strong southern drawl. "If I recollect, didn't you say something about challenging him this weekend?" The newcomer was tall—well over six feet, and broad as a barn. His white hair flared out around his head like a mane. He wore a denim team shirt that had "JJ BBQ" embroidered on the left side.

Rusty scowled at the other man. "Jack—stay out of this." Then a sly look crossed his face. "Didn't you also have some sort of argument with Bob?"

"Hell, half the people in this campground have had a falling out with Bob Woodard at one point or another," Jack replied. "I ain't nothing special there." He indicated Lili still standing frozen behind her picnic table. "Y'all need to get over yourselves about this, and not be hassling this fine lady here."

Rusty and a few of the others shot Jack a disgruntled look, but they appeared to be willing to follow his recommendation, and so the crowd in front of Lili's campground slowly dispersed, until there was only Jack, Gabby, and AJ still standing in the road.

"This your new girlfriend?" Jack said, turning to look between Gabby and AJ.

"No, Jack," Gabby said, sounding frustrated. "I only have Elanor. This is AJ Steward. She runs the Bridgewater Inn, one of the sponsors for this competition."

"Oh, nice to meet you, ma'am," Jack said, pouring on the charm.

"Nice to meet you," AJ said.

"You get hungry later, stop by Jack Jackson's BBQ for some of the best brisket you'll ever have," Jack told her earnestly.

Gabby snorted. "That's only because she hasn't tried mine yet."

"You get to be the judge of whose is best, then," he said with a broad grin. Then he paused, glancing over at Lili. "You friends with her?"

"I am," AJ said, standing up straighter.

There weren't many people who made her feel small, but Jack was on the large side—both in stature as well as personality.

"I think it's fine her being here," he said. "Shows a lot of spirit. But she's gonna be dealing with a whole bunch of idiots. Might be best if she spent the weekend at that inn of yours, instead of camping. Least 'til this is all cleared up."

"I'll mention it," AJ said.

"You do that," Jack said with a smile. "Ma'am. Gabby." He doffed an imaginary hat in their direction before heading down the road.

"Who was that?" AJ had to ask.

"Jack Jackson. He's something of a blowhard. And an asshole. However, he also has the skill to back it up. Wins most of the competitions he enters," Gabby grumbled. She walked forward, softly calling Lili's name.

AJ paused for a moment, looking after where Jack had gone.

He obviously had some sort of influence on the BBQ community, and she was glad that he'd spoken up. She'd bet that while he hadn't started the crowd, he *had* been willing to just watch until Gabby had said something.

Was he the killer?

Her gut said no. However, she'd lay money that it was someone in the crowd. Someone who'd been hassling Lili. Someone who'd set her up.

But who?

Chapter Eleven

Lili stood frozen behind her picnic table as AJ walked up. Though Gabby was saying something in a quiet voice, Lili didn't appear to be listening.

Lili glanced over at AJ, her dark eyes blank for a moment before she blinked, shook her head, and said, "I have work to do."

With that, she turned and walked over to the small cabinet next to the tent. Only then did AJ realize that the tent wasn't made out of fabric. It looked completely plastic.

Gabby turned to look at AJ, confused.

AJ just nodded. Let her handle this.

"Tell me about your tent," AJ said. "It doesn't look like a regular tent."

"It isn't," Lili said. Her words were in a complete monotone. That was one of the ways that AJ was able to tell that Lili was really upset. Instead of getting more emotional when she'd had a problem at work, she'd always gotten less so.

"What is it, then?" AJ asked.

"It's inflatable," Lili said. "I have a power blower that inflates it. It's completely waterproof and can be sealed against the elements. Which keeps it clean. The air in the sides gives it extra insulation. There's even a spot for a chimney to poke out of the ceiling, for when I want to have a heater running."

"That's pretty cool," AJ said.

Lili glanced at her. She seemed to be coming back to herself. She actually gave AJ a small smile. "It is. It's a lot less expensive than an RV, but just as sturdy and solid. It's easy for one person to set up. And clean," she emphasized again.

"You don't have a team?" AJ asked. "No one to help you?"

Lili shook her head. "I had my brother for a while, but then he got a girlfriend." She grimaced. "He tried explaining it to me, but I don't think I ever understood. Not until now." She took a deep breath. "Thank you for coming to see me this morning. It means a lot."

"Do you want me to stay with you today?" AJ asked softly.

Lili shook her head. "No, you'd just get in the way."

"I will continue to come and check on you," AJ assured her.

"I'll be making my way over to the competition area in a while," Lili said. "I was planning on doing demos of my smokers."

Gabby stepped up to talk with her about the setup she had for her equipment. They were soon going into far too many technical details for AJ to follow, about cook temperatures and times.

While many would discount Lili for her use of electronics, others would be paying her a lot of attention. Plus, the whole being-questioned-by-the-police thing had certainly made her a topic of gossip in the community.

"What are you making?" AJ asked as Lili pulled out ingredients and started her propane camp stove. Like everything else in the campsite, it looked pristine. Her logo—Precision Q—was done in cool blue and silver letters on the front.

"I brought all my sauces and rubs with me," Lili explained. "But I don't trust any of them. Plus, the police took away a bunch. So I'm remaking everything from scratch."

Lili had an electronic scale that she used to measure her ingredients before dumping them into a sauce pan. As she stirred, Gabby tried asking her about what she was doing, but Lili was barely responding.

Seemed she used some unusual ingredients, at least based on Gabby's reactions.

While AJ and Gabby stood there, another tall blond man walked by, obviously thinking about approaching them. However, Gabby just stared at him until he blanched and turned away.

"I may not be an old *abuela*, but they will respect me just the same," Gabby said. She paused, looked at Lili, then looked away again for a moment. "Lili, how do you feel about moving your campsite next to ours?"

"I—I—I would like that," Lili said quietly as she stirred her saucepan. She still wasn't looking anywhere but her stove, almost as if she were afraid to meet their eyes.

"I'll go talk with one of my neighbors," Gabby said, walking back toward her own campsite.

AJ stood watch until Gabby came back with an affirmative. They quickly helped Lili break down her camp—she emptied out the tent, deflated it, then rolled it up into a messy bundle that AJ and Gabby carried to the new site.

Once Lili was established in her new camp, AJ took her leave of them, promising to keep an eye out on Lili once she got to the contestant area. In the meanwhile, she had the next crisis to face.

Namely, meeting Bea and her mother for lunch.

Chapter Twelve

AJ was surprised at how well her mother appeared to be fitting into the town.

In fact, when she thought about it, she found it downright suspicious.

Her mom always wore her hair artfully messy, with the perfect makeup and accessories. Yet, everything today was toned down. She didn't look like some incredibly rich woman slumming in their little town. Instead, she looked more like a slightly upscale tourist. Her black jacket was from a famous designer, of course, as was her bag. But her jeans actually looked worn, her shoes had some mud on them, and her scarf appeared to be handmade. (Mind you, it probably *was* handmade, by an incredibly expensive artist in Seattle, from an exclusive art boutique.)

Bea looked the same as always, boho chic in her colorful teal-and-pink striped raincoat, her blonde hair pulled back and a cute set of white furry earmuffs. Of course, they couldn't make it three feet around the circle of BBQ contestants before Bea ran into someone else who she knew who wanted to chat with her.

Mom looked at AJ the fourth time it happened. "I take it this is a thing?"

"Always," AJ said with a nod. "Bea knows everyone in town. And at least half the tourists who regularly visit."

"Why does she keep her place in Seattle, then?" Mom asked, looking curious.

"I assume that's because Peter's practice is there, and they don't want to start from scratch down here," AJ mused.

"Oh. Right. Peter," Mom said, nodding.

AJ hid her smile. Mom had never understood Bea's relationship with her husband. They truly adored each other, even after twenty years of marriage.

"You seem to be getting along well down here as well," Mom said after a moment as Bea finished off her conversation.

"Well, I don't know *everyone* in town, unlike *some* people," AJ teased as Bea stepped back to join them. "But I have met a lot of the business owners here. And I've made friends, too." AJ had joined a woman's book club, and now had regular dinners with two of the members—Marge and Destiny.

"It is much more difficult to make friends as an adult," Mom commented.

AJ glanced at her. She seemed more thoughtful than anything else.

Then again, AJ never expected any sort of introspection from her mother.

"Why, are you thinking of moving here?" AJ said, trying for a teasing tone.

Mom scoffed. "No, I am not," she said firmly. "I just wanted to make sure that you two were doing well."

AJ caught Bea's eye at that. There was still something more going on with their mom.

Bea just shrugged. Whatever it was, she hadn't been able to learn more.

Yet.

The edges of the park were lined with tents and small trucks, where the BBQ competitors were handing out some of their food in exchange for tokens that visitors could buy at the gate. The entire area was filled with the mouthwatering scents of woodsmoke and meat. They were set just enough inland that the winds from the beach weren't constantly pushing at them, but only gusting through now and again. Bright blue sky held a sun that was warming the area. Music filled the space from the band at one end—mostly hits from the 1970s and '80s, nothing modern.

AJ, Bea, and their mom walked the entire circle, looked at the various offerings before making their choices for their first samples. One truck had BBQ chicken legs, served with a smoked peach sauce as well as a slice of roasted peach. Bea and AJ went for that, while their mother took the truck's other offering, which was a serving of pulled pork with the same peach sauce.

"How can you eat that way?" Mom complained as they sat down and AJ picked up the chicken leg. "Didn't I teach you better than to pick up a bone and just gnaw on it?"

"Sorry," AJ said, grinning as she took a deliberately large mouthful. "Must have forgotten."

Mom sighed with disgust as she carefully picked at her pork with a fork. "A little sweet," she proclaimed. "And the meat's been overcooked, something the sauce can't hide. It's dry and mushy. But it does have a nice smoke underneath."

AJ shook her head. Of course, her mom was a meat snob. Her mom was an *everything* snob.

They next went to one of the two places serving brisket that day. AJ had been assured that tomorrow there would be more samples, and they all planned on coming back and making comparisons.

The brisket didn't set her world afire, that was for certain. It was served in a meat broth, which she was certain gave it the illusion of juiciness. It was tender, though, and Mom pointed out the nice smoke ring that encircled the meat, a red ring just below the exterior.

No one commented when Lili showed up, or appeared to be giving her a hard time. AJ walked Bea and her mom over to Precision Q and listened politely to Lili and her spiel about her smokers and how they worked.

"Do you think Peter would like one of these?" Mom asked, looking at Bea.

Bea snorted. "He's not really the outdoorsy kind of guy. We don't even own a grill. Besides, I'm the one who does most of the cooking."

"So, do *you* want one?" Mom persisted. Was she angling to get a gift for Bea, as a thank you for letting her stay?

"Let me think about it," Bea said, nodding. "I'm not

going to get one unless I'm absolutely convinced that I'm going to regularly be using it."

"You might get hooked," AJ teased. "Find a new religion."

Bea just rolled her eyes at AJ.

The sisters silently communicated for a moment, with AJ indicating that she was going to stay and talk with Lili for a while and Bea should take Mom to the next stand.

After they'd left, AJ turned to Lili and asked, "How is your schedule?"

She'd learned early on in her interactions with Lili that asking how she was didn't give her any usable information. Instead, if she asked about Lili's schedule, she'd likely hear everything she needed to know.

"A little behind," Lili admitted. "Having to recreate all my sauces from scratch set me back some. As well as moving camp. But I'll be able to focus more in the new location."

"That's good," AJ said. "Anyone else come to bother you?"

That got her a quick smile. "No. Gabby's...kind of scary."

AJ was impressed that even Lili was able to recognize that. "She is," AJ said. "And she'll protect you."

Lili nodded. "Her girlfriend Elanor is lovely. I like her. It would be nice to travel with a crew again," she added wistfully.

"Maybe you can talk both your brother and his girl-friend into coming with you," AJ said.

"We tried that. While my brother gets me, his girlfriend, well, she seemed unimpressed."

"I'm sorry," AJ said. "That must have been hard."

"It was," Lili said. Then she shrugged. "So I am now going to prioritize finding someone to travel with. To make a team with."

"Good," AJ said firmly. "I think that's the right decision."

Lili gave her a shy smile. "I missed you. I missed having my choices validated."

"Here," AJ said, pulling out one of her business cards. "Call me. Or text," she added quickly, remembering how much Lili hated talking on the phone. "I'd be happy to validate your decisions at any time."

"Thank you," Lili said. She looked at the card curiously. "Psychic?" she asked.

AJ nodded. "It's currently my side-gig, though I'm hoping in another year or so, that I'll be able to do it fulltime."

Even as AJ said it, she knew that was no longer the truth. She enjoyed her time at the inn, being out from her house. Just as she enjoyed working with her psychic clients. She'd probably always spend time doing both.

Then another set of tourists came up. Lili started her spiel again about the smokers. Seemed she'd make a good commission off any she sold that weekend.

AJ slowly went back to join her mother and sister. She knew how much she'd missed Bea during the winter months, when her sister was back in Seattle. How much she'd come to rely on Roland for company, as well as the others in the circle of friends she was slowly building.

She paused for a moment, glancing at her mom.

Was that the reason why she was there? Had something happened? Not to her, but to her circle of friends? Was she looking to expand her groups somehow? Maybe down here in Milltown, despite her insistence that she wasn't moving here?

Or was something else going on?

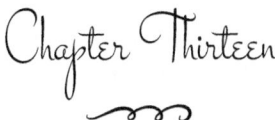

Chapter Thirteen

After they'd tried all the various BBQ vendors that were currently open, Bea announced that she was going back to the house to paint. AJ tried not to roll her eyes too hard, though she could tell that their mother was having the same impulse.

"What are you up to this afternoon?" Mom asked AJ.

"I'm, well, I have a shop to visit," AJ admitted. She still needed to get to Scents by the Sea, to talk with Naimh. "Want to walk down Main Street with me and poke your nose in all the little boutiques?"

"That sounds like fun," Mom said with a real smile.

Of course, her mother loved shopping. Much more than AJ did, as she tended to get her things online so she didn't have to deal so much with people. She had a lot of people contact already, between her clients who she did readings for and the customers at the inn. When all her work was done for the day, AJ frequently found herself wanting to be alone.

So AJ and her mom slowly walked up Main Street,

heading back into town, past the fancy condominiums on the beach, the crab shack, the other coffee shop that AJ never went to as it was too far away. Instead of Reed's Reads, there was the newly renamed Beach Reads, that was a much more appealing shop and carried a much wider, better selection of books.

Scents by the Sea turned out to be across the street from the saltwater taffy store, about midway up the strip, in one of the newer buildings. It had a single storefront window holding an impressive display of stacked, square tins, all of which contained handmade teas. The gold lettering on the black labels held intriguing names like Bedouin Nights, Starfall, Dreamless, and even a few AJ recognized like Earl Gray and Peppermint. Candles encircled the tins, all in cute glass jars, also with fun names like Orange Flights and Ocean Berries.

The shop itself wasn't very big, more of an aisle that perhaps two people could fit across. Shelves across the left wall held glass jars with hinged lids, held tight by latches. Many varieties of mixed tea were there, along with individual ingredients like stevia, lemon grass, and ginger root.

Shelves across the right wall were filled with a rainbow of candles, from pure white to midnight black. A counter stood across the back, with Naimh sitting there. Behind the counter were more shelves. Ceramic containers filled these, each precisely labeled. AJ assumed they held the more expensive ingredients. Tins of tea were also stacked there.

Smells of peppermint, lavender, licorice, and other scents teased AJ's nose as they walked in.

"Good day to ye," Naimh called out. She wore a comfortable looking gray hoodie on top of a light blue turtleneck. Her long red-gold hair was braided and worn up in a crown on the top of her head. Blue-green eyes held mischief as they gazed at AJ and her mother. It appeared that Naimh had been carefully lettering more of the stickers for her teas as she set aside a fancy gold pen.

"Hi, Naimh," AJ said, making sure to pronounce her name as *neev*, as Fred had. "I'm AJ Steward. I think we've met at a chamber of commerce meeting."

"Oh, ay," Naimh said after a moment, standing and reaching across the counter to shake AJ's hand. "Wot's the council needing?"

"Nothing," AJ said with a smile. "I'm actually here on a more personal note, to talk about herbs and like that."

"Gonna do some tasseomancy, eh?" Naimh said with a grin.

"Tasseomancy?" AJ asked, confused.

"The art of reading tea leaves, telling the future in a cup," Naimh said slyly.

"Oh," AJ said, considering. She knew nothing about that, or how that would work. She drank coffee in the mornings, though she did drink tea at night. And wine.

"It's not as traditional as scrying in a bowl o' water," Naimh added.

AJ eyebrows climbed to the top of her forehead. Seemed that Naimh knew more about her and her business than AJ knew about Naimh's.

"In a pinch, the tasseomancy might let ye see more," Naimh added.

AJ felt her mother staring holes at her back.

"That wasn't what I came in for, but I am going to think about it," AJ said honestly. "Uhm, did you hear about the person who was killed at the BBQ contest?"

Naimh snorted. "Sure did. Didn't sound like anyone's shedding any tears, either."

"I worked with the man. I think you're right," AJ admitted honestly. "However, the police are thinking a friend of mine did it, when I know she didn't."

"All right then," Naimh said with a sharp nod. "Gotta protect our own. Whatcha need?"

"According to the rumors, the victim had bright blue fingertips and lips, more than what would be caused by lack of oxygen," AJ said. "Do you know of what might cause that?"

Naimh got a sly look in her eyes again. "Don't need anything fancy here to do that. Curing salts cause that kind of look. Nitrites and nitrates. It's what they use in BBQ to make pastrami, bacon, and sausage from."

"Oh," AJ said, surprised. "I suppose that's the most obvious cause, then." Dang it! That certainly didn't narrow down any of the suspects.

"The problem with curing salts is they taste salty. Like licking a salt lick. Bitter, too. Hard to hide that taste. Don't think anyone would eat it voluntarily," Naimh said. "Now, there's others that'll do the same. Like hydrangea. Put a nice blue tint on a body. But again, nasty taste."

Naimh thought for a moment, then added, "There are plenty of poisons around that will turn skin blue from contact, not from eating. Like wolfsbane, which has such a pretty blue flower. Or foxglove. Were he wearing gloves?"

AJ considered. "A lot of the crews do wear gloves when they're preparing food. For sanitary reasons."

"It isn't the easiest way to poison someone," Naimh admitted. "Takes a while for it to build up. But, there's been more than one case of someone getting sick from foxglove. There's that one report of a gardener, wearing gloves, working with foxglove, then to take his gloves off, stuck his fingers in his mouth." Naimh's tone implied just what she thought of such an idiot.

"Maybe Bob had a box of those blue gloves, and blamed the dye in the gloves rubbing off on his finger-tips," Mom said, startling AJ. "He could have been wearing them for a while."

"That would do it," Naimh said. "Would just have to touch his face or his mouth a few times without a proper washing of his hands."

"So the police should be looking at the gloves in Bob Woodward's camp?" AJ asked.

"I would," Naimh said. "Particularly if his fingertips were blue."

That gave AJ a couple of venues to pursue. Mom bought some calming tea—with kava kava, chai spices, and licorice root—to have in the evenings.

"I'll come back and talk with you about the tasseo-mancy," AJ promised. It wasn't something she could pursue at this point, but it was something she wanted to investigate.

She sent a quick text to Roland, asking him to look

up the history of this sort of divination when he had a chance.

"So, when am I going to have a chance to meet this man of yours?" Mom asked as they started their trek up again.

"I don't know," AJ said frankly. "He knew that I'd be busy all weekend with the BBQ competition, so we didn't make any plans to be together. I did ask whether or not we could have dinner on Monday—"

"That would be lovely," Mom purred.

"But he said he'd get back to me about it," AJ continued.

Her phone rang. "Speak of the devil," she told her mom when she saw it was Roland.

"Hey beautiful," Roland said. "How's your weekend going?"

"It's okay," AJ said. "As well as can be expected with my mom here."

Her mom just rolled her eyes at that, then pointedly wandered off to look in the windows of a nearby shop, giving AJ at least the impression of privacy.

"So, tasseomancy?" Roland asked.

She could hear the grin in his voice. "Figured you needed a new topic to research, other than population migrations."

"I'll see what I can dig up, outside of the usual sources," Roland said. "Unless you want to practice on me at some point?"

"Naw, I'm still trying to decide if I even want to do it," AJ said. She had not done any sort of reading for

Roland. That felt too intimate, given the state of their relationship.

"Okay," Roland agreed easily. "What I was really calling about was dinner."

"Oh?" AJ asked. "On Monday? You can join us?"

"Yup. You think I'd give up the opportunity to meet your mom?" Roland laughed.

"You're not going to run the other direction to avoid it?" AJ teased.

Though Roland's parents lived just outside of Milltown, she hadn't been introduced. Then again, Roland didn't have the best relationship with them.

"Always good to get the difficult stuff out of the way first," Roland admitted.

That was something else AJ liked about Roland—his willingness to tackle hard things, whether it be physical or emotional work.

"So do you have a place in mind?" AJ asked. While she'd been in Milltown for a couple of years now, her budget limited her ability to go out to eat often.

"Yeah, I was going to suggest Dinkly's," Roland said.

"Oh, I've heard of that place," AJ said. She'd never met the owner—whoever it was didn't attend the regular chamber of commerce meetings, or at least not the one in Milltown. The restaurant was down the coast a ways, outside of Milltown, past the sawmills that were currently being renovated into condos.

"I've been there a few times with my parents," Roland said. "It has great steaks and beautiful sunset views of the ocean. Want me to make reservations?"

"Yes, please," AJ said. Roland's name might carry more weight and get them better seating than hers would.

"Will do," Roland said. "Any more news about the murder?"

AJ quickly filled him in with how Lili was obviously being targeted. He gave a low whistle at that.

"I'm glad she has you on her side," he said. "I wouldn't want to go against you."

"Thanks," AJ said. They hung up so he could make the reservations. He texted just a short while after that with all the details, which AJ forwarded to Bea.

Then AJ continued her walk with Mom up the street.

They stopped in Lee's Antiquities, the rock and crystal store, and a dozen others. AJ knew most of the business owners they met. A few weren't there, it being a Saturday, and they had staff who AJ didn't know.

"You seem really settled in here," Mom commented as they walked out of the gallery that sold some of Bea's paintings on commission, along with other local artists. The new owner was much more reasonable than the original had been.

"I am," AJ said. Since this was as good of an opening as she was going to get, she pressed on. "Why are you here, Mom? The real reason?"

Mom paused for a moment, looking up at AJ, slowly blinking her clear gray eyes a couple of time. "I can't just be down here to see my girls?"

"Nope," AJ said, taking the bull by the horns. "Not when you haven't bothered visiting for the past twenty years."

"But you weren't here, before," Mom said.

"Bea was," AJ pointed out.

"You never managed to come down and visit either," Mom said.

AJ opened her mouth and closed it again. Mom was right. AJ also had never taken the time to visit Bea down here in Milltown before. She'd always been working, too busy for a vacation. Plus, the sisters hadn't been as close before as they were now.

"You're right," AJ said slowly. "I didn't visit before. And I feel bad about that."

"So maybe I'm taking a page from your book and trying to make more of an effort to visit my children," Mom said. "Particularly since there's never going to be any grandchildren to spoil."

AJ nodded. She didn't feel bad about that. She'd never wanted kids and had been very clear about that from a young age. Bea had tried to get pregnant early in her marriage, but had never been successful. AJ honestly wasn't certain why.

"None of us are getting younger," Mom said determinedly. "If I want to see you, I need to make the time now."

AJ let the matter rest for the moment.

Something had happened, if not to her mom then to one of her mom's friends. Some event had worked as a wake-up call for the indomitable Irene Steward.

Did AJ really need to know what?

Or just be grateful for their time together now?

Chapter Fourteen

The Milltown police had set up a tip line for helping them catch Bob Woodward's killer. Once AJ and her mom reached her house, she left a message there about checking his gloves, to make sure that Bob hadn't been slowly poisoned over time.

"Nice place," Mom commented as she looked around the entryway. The round castle-like tower opened up just to the right of the door. AJ had left it as a comfortable seating area for clients to wait in. Instead of being closed off, AJ had opened up the area with brighter paint and lights.

"You do your psychic stuff in here?" Mom asked as AJ led her into her reading room.

"I do," AJ said. "Why, do you want a reading?"

Mom looked slightly uncomfortable at that. "No, not yet. My business is my own," she added, giving AJ a slight smile. "I don't want you finding out too much."

"Okay," AJ said. She opened her mouth then shut it again. There was something going on with her mom, but she was determined not to let AJ or Bea know what it was.

AJ found herself hesitant to leave her reading room.

She didn't have that same overwhelming urge that came upon her sometimes, when she was about to have a vision. Yet, something was going on, as while AJ led her mom on a tour through the kitchen and the second floor, she kept glancing back, looking at her reading room, as if someone were about to pop out of it.

AJ had started up the fountain again in her back yard, having turned it off over the winter. It wasn't as large as the one at the inn, standing only about three feet tall. The centerpiece was patinaed brass, made out of carved fruit and vines, the water burbling out of the top and splashing down on all sides. Roland had filled all the various planter boxes surrounding the fountain with a variety of easy-to-care-for flowers and herbs.

"You do like your water," Mom said, coming up behind AJ.

AJ nodded. She'd gone to the fountain automatically when they'd walked outside, sticking her fingers in the cold spray.

She purposefully looked away, glancing at the water out of the corner of her eye.

Nope. Nothing glowing, no shimmering fog. No vision pressing down on her.

She'd still swear that *something* was going on. Something was happening. Something that was going to require her attention. And soon.

The chirping of her cellphone instantly relieved the pressure she'd been feeling.

It was Gabby, telling her to get to back to the competition area now.

"Mom, I have to go," AJ said. "There's something that's come up with the competition. Can you get back to Bea's on your own?"

"I'll be fine," Mom said, following her back through the house and out the front door. They walked together up the short incline to Main Street, then AJ took off, letting her mom fend for herself.

It took AJ longer than she would have liked to make her way down the street, pushing through the tourist crowds. It was busier than usual on Memorial Day weekend. Was that because of the BBQ competition? AJ kind of hoped it was, as that would mean a good reason for the town to hold it once a year, that this would be the first annual.

The two women manning the gate nodded AJ through when she showed them her credentials. She was glad that she'd kept them around her neck.

She quickly made her way to the far side of the area, where Gabby stood, just outside of Lili's area.

"What is it? What's going on?" AJ asked breathlessly as she came up.

"These aren't mine," Lili said, pointing at two bottles sitting on a shelf next to her smokers. "I don't have any food down here. I won't until tomorrow. I remade all my sauces this morning. All my ingredients are up at the camp."

"So none of these are yours?" AJ said, clarifying.

"Those are," Lili said, pointing to four other bottles.

AJ noticed that none of the bottles bore any markings, no labels or other obvious signs of what they held. They were all the same size, looking like generic ketchup bottles, the tips covered in a removable top. The only thing that distinguished one from another was the color —black, white, yellow, and blue.

"Those red ones. They aren't mine," Lili said, pointing to two that were the same shade of dark red, standing beside hers.

"Did you call the police?" AJ said, looking first at Gabby, then Lili.

Gabby shook her head. "I wanted you to get here first, so you could talk with them."

"Got it," AJ said. She called Officer Brendan's personal number because she really wanted to get through to him quickly. She told him what they'd discovered and asked that he meet her at the contestant area.

It was only a few minutes before Officer Brendan and Officer Naomi arrived. They must have been on duty at the police station just a few blocks away. AJ explained the situation to them in a quiet voice, hoping to not draw too much attention to Lili and themselves.

Little luck there, as a crowd instantly surrounded them, curious onlookers wanting to know the gossip.

They did fall back when Officer Naomi gave them a good, icy glare. Then again, she had blue eyes that could freeze a body with a glance, red hair, and was built like a linebacker, with solid muscles. She was as tall as AJ— about five foot ten—and at least twice as wide.

Officer Brendan looked serious again. AJ missed his goofy smile. They took notes on what she had to tell them, took pictures of all the bottles in place, then had to confiscate all of them. Lili didn't object—she didn't trust that anything she had wasn't contaminated.

Once the police left and the crowd dispersed, Lili asked AJ in a quiet voice, "Should I drop out of the competition? How can I trust that nothing has been contaminated? I don't want to accidentally make anyone sick."

AJ sighed. She knew that Lili lived for the competition, that she took pride in her product. However, she could also understand the other woman's hesitation to continue.

"That might be for the best," AJ said. "Someone really is out to get you, if they'll come into your camp like this."

Lili nodded. Though she showed no emotion on her face, her general demeanor seemed depressed.

"If we have another BBQ contest next year, I'll make sure to waive all your fees," AJ assured her, as she didn't think there was any way to refund Lili's entrance fee. Those were paid to the LCBA, not the town.

However, next year, she was sure she could swing a deal with them.

"It's not about the money," Lili said. "I have enough." She paused and gave a faint smile. "I had a lot of stock options by the time I left."

AJ nodded. She'd cashed out early. Lili had stayed for an extra year of vesting. She probably was set for life at this point and didn't need to work if she was careful with her money.

"I don't want to be a pariah in the community," Lili said. "I work so hard to fit in. To be a part. This...this is not fair. They picked someone who was already on the outer circles."

"That was *why* they picked you," AJ said. "Because you don't have as strong allies as some of the others."

Lili sighed. "Story of my life," she muttered quietly.

"You do have Gabby on your side now. And she does have a lot of friends in the community," AJ pointed out.

"It's okay," Lili said, lifting up her chin. "I will let everyone know that I'm dropping out. They will respect me for that."

"Tell them that the reason why you're being picked on is because you're certain you could have won this contest," AJ told her. "That it's jealousy."

Lili blinked. "But that isn't the truth," she said.

"How do you know?" AJ shot back. "There might be some sort of jealousy involved."

"Hmmm," was all that Lili had to say. "Can you stay here for a few minutes while I go and withdraw from the competition? All I'll do is talk to people about the smokers for the rest of the event. I won't turn in any meats."

"Happy to stay here for you," AJ said. She was also determined to let Fred Hanson know about her ploy, to get the rumor spread that Lili was being targeted for the quality of her BBQ.

After Lili had gone, AJ sat behind Lili's tables and watched the people walking by. A few of the other contestants casually walked by, like Rusty, though he didn't stop. At least he'd put on a clean shirt for dealing with the public. AJ texted a note to Gabby about still needing to hear the entire story behind him.

Another man stopped by, someone who could have been Bob Woodward's cousin, given his pale skin, receding hairline and chin line, as well as his glacier blue eyes. However, he introduced himself as Albert and a friend of Gabby's. He and his friend Paulo ran Smoking Good Q, and that they'd be happy to help Lili if she needed anything.

AJ was very touched that at least some of the community was rallying around Lili. And that she might have more friends than she realized, though they did come from Gabby.

The next person who came up was another contestant. His shirt proclaimed him part of the Ruling Quartet BBQ. The words encircled what AJ supposed were tiny embroidered representations of the four primary meats that were turned in at most BBQ competitions—brisket, pulled pork, chicken and ribs.

"Hi! I'm Gilbert. King of the competition," he said as he came walking up, sticking his hand out.

"Hi, I'm AJ," she said, standing slowly and taking the proffered hand. He gave her a firm shake, not too hard but not too soft, either.

"And who proclaimed you as king?" AJ had to ask.

Sure, he was almost as handsome as Payne Thomas, with beautiful flowing blond hair that waved down to his shoulders, pretty green eyes, a hero's cleft chin and jawline, a modest sprinkling of cute freckles across a proud nose, and shoulders that went on for days. He'd look good with a crown, maybe a royal blue cape, and a scepter.

AJ instantly didn't trust him.

"You'll see when the meats are turned in," he said with a wink. "Now, I heard that there was some issue here with Lili."

"If you know Lili, you'll also know that she didn't do it," AJ shot back.

"True, true," Gilbert said, nodding and looking thoughtful.

AJ could practically feel him turn his charm dial up to eleven as he focused on her. Those green eyes beheld her. Nothing else in the world mattered as much as she did. No one else was as important.

It would take most women's breath away.

However, she wasn't sixteen, or even twenty-six, and easily influenced.

Plus, while she didn't know if this Gilbert was using magic on her or not, her own magic welled up and washed away whatever influence he was trying to exert.

AJ crossed her arms over her chest and glared at the man. "You want something. What is it?"

Gilbert blinked in surprise. He didn't physically take a step back, but AJ knew he was mentally adjusting his stance.

She was supposed to answer any and all of the questions he asked. She'd swear to it.

He wasn't used to women saying no to him.

Too bad.

"I was just curious, what do we know about the poison used on Bob?" Gilbert asked, still sounding cautious. "Was it injected? Was it swallowed? Or was it administered by contact?"

"We don't know," AJ said frankly. There had been a

lot of speculation about what exactly had been the cause of Bob Woodward's death. Until the formal autopsy came back, no one would really know.

"They said his fingertips were bright blue," Gilbert pressed. "That implies contact."

AJ nodded. "Or nitrites and nitrates."

"Not bright blue," Gilbert said. "They produce more of a bluish-brown color. No, I was thinking about hydrangeas."

"Oh?" AJ asked. Hadn't Naimh mentioned those?

"Yup. Or larkspur, though it really isn't the season for those," Gilbert mused, his eyes far off. "I study plants. And herbs," Gilbert admitted after a few moments, looking back at AJ. "It's why my BBQ is so successful. I know just the right amount of secret spices to put into my sauces."

"I see," AJ said.

"You be sure to come by and have a taste later," Gilbert said. "Nice to meet you."

After a casual wave he strode off, back into the crowd.

Interesting.

She texted Gabby a note, telling her that they should talk about Gilbert as well.

Could he be the killer? He had tried to charm her. Maybe he'd unsuccessfully tried to charm Bob Woodward as well.

Dang it! That left her with more suspects and even fewer answers than she'd had before.

AJ sighed and hoped that the path forward would become clear sooner rather than later.

Chapter Fifteen

As the evening wore down, AJ went back to the campgrounds with Gabby so they could talk in private.

Elanor prepared the pork butts while Gabby started stoking up the fires in Inez, their smoker. AJ had no idea of all the prep work that went into meat, between trimming it to perfection, injecting it, as well as seasoning it.

Las Chicas would smoke four pork butts. However, they would only turn in a handful of meat to the judges. This was why there would be so much BBQ available for the general public to taste on Sunday, after the contestants started turning in their product.

That was actually the same case with all of competition meats: they prepared a lot and only sent in the best of the best to the judges. Cooking four briskets and only sending in six slices. Preparing two dozen chicken thighs and only being judged on six of them. Ribs, too.

Elanor kicked them both out of the RV while she finished prepping the pork, insisting on doing it by herself. AJ pulled up a camp chair and wrapped a handy blanket around herself while Gabby tended the flames.

"I always have to start with a real fire," Gabby said into the quiet night. The sun had set, and the air was chilled. "I don't know why. You'd think that if I started the fire magically that it would be easier to control magically for the rest of the night. But for whatever reason, despite the fact that it's a real fire burning real wood, a fire that's started magically goes through peaks and troughs that aren't explained by whatever I'm feeding it."

"Could that be so that it doesn't burn out of control?" AJ mused. "If it dies down naturally, you won't be burning down an entire forest?"

Gabby shrugged as she continued to load more sticks of firewood into the firebox that was set to one side of the smoker.

Inez looked like two big black oil drums that had been welded together end to end, then set on their sides. Hinged doors were set into the middle of both drums, a chimney stuck up on the right, and a large, rectangular box on the left. The idea was for the smoke to travel from the fire box on the one side, across the meat in the center, then up out of the chimney. Large pans of water rested under the meat grates inside the drums to keep everything moist. Thermometers were set into the hinged doors, but Gabby also had probes sticking into the meat that she could monitor.

AJ had seen many smokers that weekend, most of them painted. There was even one that looked like a small, green, military tank. It was controlled remotely and moved around on treads. Inez was one of the few that was pure black with no logo on the side.

"She's a dark lady," Gabby had explained earlier in the week when AJ had asked about the lack of markings. "She rarely shows her colors to anyone. But they are there, if you know what to look for."

AJ watched as the temperatures inside the old offset smoker started to rise. Maybe it was her imagination, but she thought she saw a hint of red-gold starting to encase the metal.

Finally, the pork butts were on the grill, timers were set, and Elanor went back inside the RV so that AJ and Gabby could talk. They sat side by side on camp chairs in front of Inez. There wasn't much heat wafting off her—she was insulated so the heat stayed inside the smoker.

"Tell me about Rusty Thomas," AJ started off with.

Gabby gave her a wicked smile. "There was this reality TV show—*The Q Clash*—where competitors had to cook all these crazy things on smokers and grills and such. And they had to do it in such a short time frame. I mean, on one show? They cooked brisket in five hours. That's like, insane!"

"I'll take your word for it," AJ said with a smile.

"Seriously, like, brisket takes six to eight hours just to cook! And then you should rest it. I get the best results resting for another four hours. I still don't know how they managed to get a good product out of only five hours, total," Gabby said, shaking her head.

"So what happened to Rusty? Was he on this show?" AJ said. She'd learned that she needed to keep Gabby focused sometimes, particularly when it came to talking about BBQ.

"He was on the first season. So was Bob Woodward, as a judge. They didn't get along," Gabby said. "I mean, sure, after the show they said that it was all just for TV and that they'd made up. Like, they were besties now. It was bullshit. They hated each other. It was obvious on the show, as well as afterward."

"Like when they were at the same competition?" AJ said.

"That, and their Birdy accounts. They were always sniping at each other."

AJ made a note to go and check their social media accounts. That sort of thing had helped her figure out who had killed the other psychic in town.

"Could Rusty have killed Bob?" AJ asked.

Gabby sighed. "I don't know. Lots of people hated Bob. And Rusty, well, he's always struck me as something of a coward."

"Was Bob going to be judging this contest?" AJ said.

"I think so, but it wouldn't have mattered," Gabby said. "The judging is all done blind. The people who are tasting the meats have no idea who prepared it. That's why it takes so long to prep the box that's going to the judges. You need it to look a certain way, so that it will stand out on its own merits, and the meat will be enticing, not because it looks different than the other boxes."

"Do you think Bob would have been able to figure out which boxes were Rusty's anyway?"

"It still wouldn't have mattered. Not every judge tastes every product. Not unless Bob had completely circumvented the entire process, and I don't think he would have done that. Not even for Rusty, no matter how much they might have hated each other," Gabby said.

AJ sighed. She didn't want to let go of Rusty as a suspect. She had a feeling about him. However, Gabby knew these people better than she did. If Gabby didn't consider him a prime suspect, AJ wouldn't either.

"What about this Gilbert character?" AJ said, setting Rusty to the side for the moment. She lowered his voice. "Does he have magic?"

Gabby grimaced. "No, not as far as I can tell. Or if he does, it's so weak that I can't find it."

AJ explained about him turning on the charm, and how it felt as if her magic had risen up to wash it away.

"Hmmm," Gabby said. "You know, I felt the same way, as if my fires burned his influence away. But I didn't feel anything magical about what he did. Here," she said.

She got out of her chair, opened the firebox, and did...*something* to the fire. AJ couldn't see what.

However, she could *feel* it. Gabby had used her magic on the flames. AJ had no doubt about that at all.

Gabby looked over at AJ, who nodded. "All right, I understand," AJ said. "Gilbert didn't do anything that felt like magic."

"Exactly," Gabby said as she sat back down. "He just has this charisma and some control over it. I don't know what that ability is. He's always charming. Just sometimes, there's an extra oomph to it."

"He was asking about the poison that had been used on Bob," AJ said.

Gabby raised an eyebrow at her. "Did he, now? That's interesting."

"He said he was familiar with a lot of herbs and spices, which was why he always won contests," AJ continued.

Gabby snorted. "Jack Jackson would have something to say about that. He wins more. Almost everything he enters. No magic there either." She sighed. "Jack's an asshole. Opinionated. Loud mouth. Uncouth. But…he knows how to cook BBQ. And he works hard at it."

AJ sensed that Gabby had a grudging respect for Jack Jackson. "So what about Gilbert? And his spices? He was asking specifically about hydrangeas. And larkspur."

"I don't know," Gabby said. "He might have been showing off. It wouldn't surprise me if he had knowledge of poison. But that seems a little blatant to me, to just come up and ask you about it."

"Maybe he thought his charm would hold my tongue," AJ pointed out.

"Maybe," Gabby said. "We should check his social media accounts, too, and see if we can figure out his relationship with Bob Woodard."

AJ nodded and took another note on her phone. The campsite was basically a black hole in terms of cellphone reception, so she couldn't check anything now.

"I wish I could contact my aunt. My bio-dad's sister," Gabby said after a bit. "She knows more about poisons than just about anybody. But she disappeared a few years ago."

AJ had learned a little of Gabby's background—that her bio-dad was some sort of Mexican drug lord and her mom had escaped to California with the girls when they were very young. Her mom had found and married the man they considered their dad shortly thereafter. However, Gabby had mentioned that some of her bio-dad's relatives had sought her out once she'd started practicing her magic.

"If you want to talk with someone about poison, there's Naimh in town," AJ suggested, as she'd already told Gabby about her conversation with the woman.

Gabby nodded. "I'm sure she knows a lot, particularly about what grows native here," she said. "But she probably hasn't made a serious study of poisons. Unlike my aunt."

AJ just shrugged, but she had to agree. Naimh had known about toxic plants, but probably didn't employ them.

From Gabby's statement, AJ wondered how much of her aunt's knowledge about poison was practical, not theoretical.

"So who else could be a suspect?" AJ asked.

She and Gabby started going through all the BBQ teams, and AJ had a whole list of people to check out on social media later that evening.

As AJ was getting ready to go, Cecilia insisted that AJ try some of their practice chicken. Though Elanor complained that it wasn't tender enough, the skin still melted on AJ's tongue and the meat was so moist and delicious.

They sent her home with a box full of "inadequate" chicken thighs and more questions than answers, along with promises to talk more in the morning.

Chapter Sixteen

AJ opened the front door to her house and stopped in the doorway.

Someone was there.

She didn't know how she knew, but she did.

"Hello?" she called out, unwilling to take another step.

When no reply immediately came, she started fumbling for her phone.

"Is that you, AJ?" came a familiar alto.

"Mom?" AJ said, relief cascading down her shoulders. "Is that you?"

"And me!" Bea added.

AJ rolled her eyes as she took a deep breath and released it, sighing it out. It was a technique she'd learned to help her relax. It was particularly good when she needed to calm down before doing a client reading.

"What are you doing here?" AJ called out as she took off her coat.

"Didn't you get my text?" Bea said.

AJ finally dug out her phone. As she was swiping it on, it pinged at her, letting her know that she'd received a message.

"Just now," AJ snorted as she picked up her box of chicken thighs and walked through the front room to the back, where her kitchen sat.

She was not surprised to see Bea and their mom at the small kitchen table with a swath of cut-up raw veggies, what looked like an assortment of cold cuts, and two glasses of wine with the contents half gone.

"Let me get another chair," AJ said as she weighed the box in her hand.

"Oh, what's that?" Bea asked.

"Practice chicken from Las Chicas," AJ admitted. "Elanor claims that the cook isn't good enough for judging."

"We should be the judge of that," Bea said, snagging the box from AJ. When AJ held onto it for a moment, Bea continued. "What, you weren't planning on sharing? Even after we'd brought you food?"

"Well, I suppose," AJ said, relinquishing her prize. "Since you did actually tell me you were on your way over, though you didn't bother to get a reply from me."

"I knew you'd be working until all hours," Bea said with a dismissive wave of her hand. "You'd appreciate having dinner already prepared."

AJ nodded. Her sister actually did know her well.

She went and snagged one of the folding chairs in the front hall that she had for clients and carried it back to the kitchen.

As she walked into the kitchen, she once again

appreciated how cozy the place felt. The undercounter lighting was perfect in terms of making if bright enough to see by but not glaring. Pops of color also brightened the area, like the red bread box, her teal tea pot, and the bright yellow salt and pepper shakers. Clean black and white tile on the floor gave the room a more old-fashioned feel, while the white cabinets, black countertops, and all new stainless steel appliances made it more modern.

The three of them chatted amicably, Mom talking about the shops she'd discovered, Bea doing a bit of rambling about the painting she'd just finished, and AJ telling them about what had happened that afternoon, leading up to Lili withdrawing from the contest, then giving them a rundown on who might be potential suspects.

Mom put down her wine glass and shook her head at her daughters. "You two don't need to solve this, you know. Let the police handle it."

"But Lili's my friend," AJ pointed out. "And she isn't the easiest person to be around. She's somewhere on the autism spectrum. Difficult to talk to, or to figure out what she's saying, sometimes."

Mom gave her a calculating look. "You frequently rooted for the underdog as a teenager. Instead of sticking to your guns and aligning yourself with the top dog."

AJ shrugged. She remembered her mother being disappointed with her frequently, telling her that she wasn't living up to her potential. That memory no longer stung as much, particularly since her "potential" and the direction of her life had changed so much.

"All right, then what do we need to do?" Mom said. "Since you two are so determined to go down this path?"

AJ blinked, surprised. "What, you want to help?"

Mom gave her a sly smile. "Sure. Why not? Might be fun. A way to learn something about these people."

AJ glanced over at Bea, who just shrugged.

Yeah, neither of them were certain of their mother's angle.

However, AJ trusted that all would be made clear eventually.

She got out a notebook and copied out all the names she'd written down on her phone from her talk with Gabby. Then they divided the names into three groups, one for each of them.

It didn't surprise AJ that her mom knew all the ins and outs of social media. Crafting an image took place on many platforms these days. And her mom had always been concerned about how she appeared to the public.

"Which platforms do you advertise on?" Mom asked AJ as she looked at her list.

"For the psychic business? I don't do online readings, so I mainly do in person ads, in the local newspaper, putting up fliers in local businesses, and so on. I do some advertising on chamber of commerce pages, so that when tourists are looking at the town, they'll also see my business," AJ said, trying not to get defensive.

"I'm on all of the platforms," Bea announced. "I do visual art. And online sales. It makes more sense for me to be active in that way than AJ."

"Hmmm," was all Mom replied, obviously not satisfied with AJ's answer but not digging in more.

They checked the Birdy site, with all the chirps there, as well as the other social media platforms.

AJ found she couldn't do a general search on Bob Woodward. Since his death, a lot of people had been posting stories about him, so he was being mentioned everywhere.

She had to actually find people's accounts and look at their general timelines in order to figure out their relationship with Bob.

Fortunately, none of his accounts had been deleted yet. Based on what she read, he appeared to spend at least half of his time online arguing with various people.

Plus, though people claimed to have good memories of him, based on the number of conversations that he had, less than a quarter of the people with whom he regularly interacted were saying nice things about him, how they'd miss him. Most people weren't saying anything at all.

AJ had given Rusty's account to her mom, as she figured she'd be the least biased of all of them. AJ knew that she'd be looking for a way to make him guilty, at least unconsciously. Better that someone less biased look at him.

She did keep Gilbert for herself, though. Just before she started poring over his social media, she sent a text to Lili asking about him, figuring that she'd hear from Lili in the morning, when she left the camp and had cell phone access again.

Lili replied immediately, though. Of course, she would have some sort of booster to be able to stay connected to the outside world.

*Gilbert has only grown interested
in me since the police came by*

AJ frowned and told Bea and their mom about that.

"I would advise her to stay away from him, since he expressed so much interest in the poison," Bea said flatly.

AJ did so, only to be told that Gabby had already sent Gilbert packing.

AJ snorted at that. She had no idea what Gabby had done to Gilbert when he'd come by that evening, but she'd probably made him very uncomfortable. Not that she'd set his private parts on fire, though Gabby might have been tempted.

While the feeds of some of the other contestants primarily consisted of pictures of raw and cooked meat, Gilbert's social media accounts had a lot (*a lot*) of selfies in them. Always with that same sly smile, eyes crinkling at the corners, lips soft and kissable. It showed him at many different BBQ contests, but never the other people on his team, the prizes they won, or their products.

Just him.

AJ shook her head. Maybe he thought that the "personal touch" was the way to sell themselves to the crowds, since the competitors may or may not cover their contest expenses with prize money. AJ had learned that the BBQ teams made money through sponsorships (like Lili and the smokers she sold), through selling their own spice rubs and sauces, or by driving business to their restaurant or food truck.

The competition expenses were advertising dollars more than anything else.

"Who's that?" Bea asked, looking over AJ's shoulder.

"Gilbert," AJ said, and explained about what he'd done.

"Too pretty," was their mom's comment. "And pretty, while it may last longer in a man, won't last forever."

AJ snorted. Yup. He was too pretty. Was he a killer? He seemed too vapid and self-absorbed to care about anybody else enough to want to kill them. His interactions with Bob Woodward were mild to say the least. As far as AJ could tell, while they knew each other, Gilbert never interacted with the other man much. They hadn't had the arguments that littered Bob's feeds. Unless it had all been through private messages, but Bob appeared to like to bring a spotlight to whatever ruckus he was raising.

With a sigh, AJ put Gilbert to the side and started following up on other leads.

There was another woman named Kayleigh—the lead of the Rain City Meats team—who appeared to have it out for Bob, her feeds filled with caustic barbs the pair of them tossed at one another.

However, though Rain City Meats was on AJ's list of competitors, there was a big cancellation notice on their feed about how they hadn't been able to make it to the Sandy Point competition due to a death in the family.

They didn't have any mention of Bob's death on their feed, either Kayleigh's or the team's feed.

AJ tried not to feel disappointed. That meant one less suspect, right?

"Huh," Mom said, distracting AJ from digging into

the next team. "Did you know that some people are allergic to ibuprofen?"

"No," AJ said, a little confused. "Who are you looking up?"

"A, uh, Rusty Thomas. Seems he's allergic to it, and was posting some sort of PSA to parents about it. Some people seemed skeptical. Then, Bob Woodward pops in and mentions that he, too, is allergic to it."

"What happens during a reaction? Do your fingers and lips turn blue?" AJ asked.

"Causes heart palpitations, and can lead to heart attack," Mom said after a moment.

"Well, heart attack can cause your lips and fingers to turn blue," Bea said. "Can't it?"

"That's after the fact," AJ said. "Not before. And probably not bright blue."

"So maybe there was something that was slowly killing him, turning his fingers blue, and then someone else decided to speed up the process?" Mom suggested.

"A whole lot of people didn't like him," AJ admitted.

By the end of the evening, AJ still had more questions, and possible suspects, than she had answers.

At least she also had some mighty fine chicken, even if it wasn't "competition worthy."

Chapter Seventeen

Despite the amount of wine that AJ had consumed with Mom and Bea, she still got up early and took herself out for a swim. The sky was clear and a definite chill hung in the air. Water sparkled in the distance as she walked out of her house, already encased in her warm wetsuit, goggles pressing tightly against her forehead.

As always, AJ left a text for Bea telling her sister that she was going swimming. Though AJ had no fear of the water—it was her element—she still knew better than to take her abilities for granted. There wasn't anything Bea could do if AJ drowned, but at least her sister would know what had happened if AJ disappeared.

As she walked across the fine sand, her water shoes sinking into the earth before she made her way to firmer surfaces, she had a stray thought about how that would be the perfect way to fake a death. A strong swimmer disappearing after telling someone they'd gone into the ocean.

Maybe she'd have to mention that to Fred, and he could use it in his next murder mystery...

AJ left a towel and her phone on the sand close to the water, along with a bright orange flag on a tall plastic pole that she could see from far away. There wasn't any magic in the flag, but she always dipped it in the ocean before she planted it, so it was coated in water, at least until the wind blew it dry. The flag helped her find her starting point if she got caught in an unexpected current and traveled further away than she'd planned.

After stretching a little and doing a few jumping jacks to warm herself up, AJ raced from the shore into the water, plowing into the waves and not bothering to dive under until she was at least thigh-deep. The cold struck her more as bracing than chilling, waking her all the way up.

With sure, strong strokes, AJ left the constant waves and churn closer to the shore and headed out. She knew from experience—as well as her own magical senses—where the floor of the ocean suddenly dropped away and the water grew calmer. Sure, there were dangerous currents out this far. She still needed to be careful. But the water felt wonderful to her, safe and inviting.

AJ swam up and down several times, parallel to the shore—a form of doing laps—relishing the feeling of the water surrounding her, the buoyancy of her body, how she felt as though she was sliding through the water like a knife.

It wasn't necessarily physically easy. She built up a sweat even in the cold, and her muscles grew pleasantly tired. AJ paused for a moment, treading water, marking where her flag and her house were.

Should she go in? She shouldn't exhaust herself today. She had to meet Mom and Bea for brunch in a while, then go to the BBQ competition. Hopefully nothing had happened overnight that would need her immediate attention.

But she loved being out on the water, the way it held her, how the lights sparkled against the waves...

AJ gasped.

Crap.

That light. Once she focused on it, it started to wend its way toward her, weaving across the top of the little waves like a glowing snake.

AJ didn't think she could outswim it, not with how fast it was moving.

She knew, though, that it was carrying a vision that would overtake all her senses once the light touched her.

She readied herself, treading water as the light drew closer.

The light turned from white to pure gold as soon as it reached her. AJ felt herself covered in gold sparkles, as if the light had turned itself into rain.

The brightness made her close her eyes.

Then she began to see...

The first image was a small blue robot. It was roughly man-shaped, though its arms, legs, torso, and head were all different sized blocks. Bright yellow blobs made up the hands and feet. Though they weren't articulated, the robot appeared to have no difficulty picking things up or walking. Its eyes were pure black squares surrounded by more yellow.

AJ recognized where the robot was working—it was in a campsite, hanging out in its own small tent. People walked by and the robot watched them with its flat face. It barely came up to the knees of most everyone.

AJ couldn't read the emotions of the robot. Was it happy to be left alone? Sad? Lonely? Or content? The whole scene seemed very flat.

The robot pulled open a can clearly marked as oil, then it started sipping the brownish-red liquid.

While the robot's movements hadn't been that smooth, they abruptly grew shaky, as if its gears were grinding together. It didn't take too long before the robot fell over to the side. Black X's crossed over its eyes.

Only then did AJ get a look at the can of oil. Sitting at the bottom of it was a rusting piece of iron. It had a dull tip but a large head, more like a railway spike.

The robot had been poisoned.

AJ found herself being drawn into the can of oil. The smell of the chemical filled her nose. It reminded her of how Roland smelled sometimes, after he'd been working a mower all day. The bitter taste rolled across her tongue. Cold shivers ran across her shoulders.

She found herself reaching for that piece of iron, though a part of her knew that she needed to let it go. She'd seen what had happened. Reaching for more wouldn't be good.

However, AJ was stubbornly determined to grab hold of that piece of metal. She felt as though if she could touch it, she would *know* who the killer was, who'd placed it so carefully in the robot's only source of substance.

It was so close. Just a fraction of an inch away. If she had longer fingernails, she could scrape them across it.

Suddenly, she was drowning in the oil. It sloshed over her head, pushing her down, not buoying her up. She tried to breathe but there was no air. Flailing, she struck out with hands and feet, searching for the side or bottom of the can. Nothing was in reach, now. She was stuck in a dark morass that weighed heavily on her limbs and was starting to crush her.

Instead of continuing to flail in the dark, AJ reached for her magic. There wasn't much water in the oil. Just the tiniest amount. She couldn't care about the railroad spike anymore. She had to get out.

Now.

Fortunately, oil and water don't mix. Particularly agitated water.

AJ shot straight up, out of the can, landing with a plop back in the ocean, where she'd started.

She found herself panting as she took deep breaths of air. She held her head back, floating with her face up toward the sky. She coughed a bit, though she didn't feel like she'd swallowed any water.

Had she started drowning? Unable to keep herself afloat as the vision overtook her?

The water around her held her up in a reassuring fashion. Slowly, AJ calmed.

How much of what she'd felt of her drowning had been real? And how much of it had been her grasping for things beyond her reach in the vision?

A familiar headache bloomed behind her eyes.

Crap.

She had *really* pushed herself too hard. Whenever she tried to do too much with her psychic abilities, her head let her know, loud and clear.

With a groan, AJ started slowly swimming back toward shore.

It was obvious who the robot was. Lili. Someone was out to get her.

However, what had been that piece of metal that had killed her? Was it a railroad spike? Just a nail? Who did that represent?

And could AJ warn Lili in time to save her?

Chapter Eighteen

As soon as AJ reached the beach, she called Lili.

"Lili! Where are you and what are you doing?" She realized she sounded breathless and kind of crazed. There was no helping that, though.

"I'm at the campsite with Gabby and Cecelia," Lili said slowly.

"Can I talk with Gabby?"

Suddenly Gabby was on the line.

"What's up?"

AJ explained about her vision to Gabby, though the words came slowly as she calmed some and her headache expanded.

"I'll make sure she understands that she can only eat the food that Las Chicas prepares," Gabby assured AJ.

"Thanks," AJ said. She was so glad that Gabby had been there, that she hadn't had to try to explain a vision to Lili. Who was not about to believe her.

AJ walked slowly up to her house, her legs leaden. She felt awful and her head was killing her.

Nothing would touch a headache brought on by overusing her abilities. Resting in a dark room with a cold beanbag over her eyes made her feel better, but the pain would remain. Caffeine helped slightly, though it might just be her focusing on other things rather than how awful she felt.

However, AJ couldn't just take the day off. Her mom was there, in Milltown, obviously intending to spend as much time with her children as she could. Plus, AJ had things she had to do as part of the chamber of commerce for the contest. She couldn't just crawl into her bed and sleep for the day, no matter how much she might want to.

So AJ showered, did what she could to make herself look better (though she was unimpressed with the results) and pinged Bea, telling her that she'd be late to brunch.

You bringing Roland?

AJ rolled her eyes at Bea's reply.

No. We're going out to dinner
Monday, remember?

She could practically hear Bea's sigh from where she was standing.

Fine. C U then

Bea's texts had gotten a little better in terms of misspellings. She'd found a new voice-to-text app. It did, though, tend to abbreviate what it could to mere letters.

AJ took her time leaving her house and walking up the short incline to Main Street. The crowds were already out and about. She was glad they'd made reservations at Gladstones, the swanky restaurant where they were meeting for brunch.

Even though the restaurant was only a couple blocks away, AJ still stopped in the Storm Brew Café for a small coffee to hold her over. AJ felt like praising the heavens when she saw that Juli was working that weekend. She tended to work only during the weeks, leaving the crazy weekend traffic to the other baristas. However, it was a holiday, and so everyone was working.

Juli had let her hair grow out over the winter and hadn't shaved it short again, so her entire scalp was covered in short, dirty blonde hair that had been artfully twisted into tiny spikes all over. Unadorned gold rings pierced her eyebrow, nose, and bottom lip. Tattoos covered most of her right arm, the full sleeve still being filled in.

The cheerful barista took one look at AJ and asked, "Double or triple shot this morning?"

AJ would have laughed, but her head hurt too much. "Double, as I'll get more coffee shortly. Mocha, please. With extra whipped cream."

"You got it," Juli said. "I'd ask how you are doing, but you look like you need to save your strength instead."

"Thanks," AJ said. She pointed to the pretty blue flower that was just above Juli's wrist. "That just get filled in?"

"It did!" Juli said proudly as she passed the order down the line to Kenny, the other person working the big espresso machine that morning. "It represents tranquility and harmony, reminding me to seek out peace, and to remember to breathe."

"Cool," AJ said. All of the tattoos that Juli had represented her personal mythology, many of them working as reminders either of past events or as touchstones for her everyday living.

As Juli took the order of the next person in line, AJ stepped to the side, waiting for her drink. While Juli was the best barista, Kenny was at least adequate. And sure enough, as soon as all the customers had their orders in, Juli stepped up to the machine and started slinging drinks, moving much faster than her coworker.

AJ was grateful that Juli was the one who actually made her mocha. Though the barista didn't have any magic, AJ was convinced that her sunny disposition contributed to the drinks she created, making everything taste better.

AJ hurriedly dug her sunglasses back out of her purse as she walked down the street, nectar of the gods in hand. It was just too dang bright, and she just wasn't in the mood to interact with anyone. Fortunately, people kept out of her way, though she did have to step into the street to get around the family of five—two adults and three very young children—who insisted on walking shoulder to shoulder.

At least AJ wasn't too late when she arrived at Gladstones. It was on the second floor of the Callaghan building, and it faced the back of the building, with windows all across that looked out over the ocean. During the off-season they were only open for breakfast and lunch, but during the on-season they also hosted sunset-viewing parties, with a menu featuring light appetizers and drinks. The hours varied, depending on when the sun was setting.

Though there was a long line, AJ slipped into the restaurant, finding that Bea and Mom were already seated with a pitcher of what was surely mimosas on the table.

"You okay?" Bea asked as AJ slid into her seat.

"Yeah," AJ said as she quaffed the rest of the mocha from the Storm Brew Café. She knew it was gauche to bring outside food into a restaurant. But she'd really needed that initial hit.

"Rough night," AJ told them when she realized that both Bea and her mom were silently staring at her.

"We didn't drink that much, did we?" Mom asked, looking from Bea to AJ and back again. "I mean, I certainly don't have the tolerance I once did, but you two should be fine."

"No, it wasn't the wine last night," AJ said, trying to smile though she wasn't certain her face moved that way at the present time. "Or the whining," she added, with a very direct look at Bea.

"What? Just because we brought you dinner didn't mean you had to set us to work all night," Bea grumped.

AJ rolled her eyes.

"So what happened?" Mom asked quietly. "Why do you look as though you haven't slept in a week and you're coming off of a particularly bad bout of flu?"

"Do I look that bad?" AJ asked Bea.

Bea shrugged. "I've seen you look worse. You know. Like right after you started your psychic business."

AJ nodded, grimacing. She'd really, *really* pushed her psychic powers too much that time. It had taken almost a month for her to recover.

"It won't be that bad this time," AJ said, mainly for Bea's sake.

Her sister narrowed her eyes. "You saw something."

AJ felt her own eyes grow wide. She looked from Bea to their mom and back again. "Uhm..."

"Bea said you were having visions," Mom said quietly.

AJ glared at Bea. "You're dead to me."

Her sister just shrugged. "Great Aunt Loraine evidently also had visions. Or at least one vision. Right?" she said, turning to their mother.

"Possibly. I didn't really remember until the other day, when we were talking about it. I must have been a teenager, sixteen, seventeen, at the time. Great Aunt Loraine was visiting, and she put up quite a fuss one night about me staying in with her instead of going out with my friends. I think that was the night she also taught me how to play poker."

Mom took a sip of her mimosa before she continued. "My friends got into a pretty bad car accident that night. Skidded off the highway and ran into a tree. Most of the damage was done to the back door on the passenger side. There were only three people in the car. None of them were sitting in that seat. If I'd been along, would I have been sitting there? Injured? Or maybe killed?" She gave a visible shudder.

"Great Aunt Loraine said it was just coincidence, that she'd been lonely. But I remember how satisfied she looked. And I always wondered why she'd made such a fuss. Normally, she was really easy to get along with."

"So when Mom told me about that, and she seemed okay with it, I told her that yes, sometimes, you see things as well," Bea continued.

AJ just shook her head. Honestly, Bea should have checked with her first before saying anything to their mom. However, they could have that argument later.

"So this morning, I might have had a vision about Lili being poisoned," AJ said quietly. "I've already talked with Gabby and we've taken care of it."

"Why would anyone want to poison the person who the police think might have been the killer?" Bea asked, puzzled.

AJ just shrugged. Her head hurt too much for her to try to figure that out.

Mom snorted. "Isn't it obvious?" She looked from one to the other. "If Lili dies, and then the police find a suicide note, the real killer won't have any fingers pointing at them anymore. Chances are, no one will investigate any further."

AJ opened her mouth to claim that the police would keep looking into the matter, then closed it. Officers Naomi and Brendan, along with Sheriff Cavallo, were good enough for Milltown, but they weren't real detectives. If they couldn't figure out who'd done it, they might have to bring in outside help.

If they could find a plausible suspect, albeit dead, they might stop looking. No matter what AJ had to say in the matter.

"So what do we do? Should we tell Lili to leave town?" Bea asked.

"No," AJ said, resisting the urge to shake her poor aching head. "Whoever the killer is, they don't have to kill her here. They might wait until the next BBQ competition. Or the one after that. They just have to see an opportunity and take it."

"Lili could quit going to competitions," Mom pointed out.

"Bea, how would you feel if someone told you that you could no longer paint?" AJ replied.

Bea shuddered. "I'd rather die."

"That's why Lili can't quit competitions," AJ told Mom.

"I see," Mom said quietly.

She didn't—she'd never had a passion like Bea's. However, she did understand the comparison.

Food arrived shortly after that and AJ devoured her "green eggs and ham"—a traditional eggs benedict served with a good helping of spinach. The hollandaise sauce had just the right amount of tang, the English muffins still had a nice toastiness to them, the spinach had been wilted with a little lemon and garlic, and the eggs were the perfect consistency, the runny yolks lending more creamy goodness to every bite.

AJ had things to do at the competition starting at noon. The three of them wouldn't be getting back together until two PM, when the contestants would start serving their "leftover" competition meats.

As they dawdled over coffee, Mom asked AJ, "So

what exactly did you see? And are you always this wiped out after one of them?"

AJ grimaced, still not happy that her mom knew that she sometimes had visions. "Visions come in two categories. The ones that are composed of symbols indicate something in the future that can be changed. Visions that contain real people, generally dead people, can't be changed."

"And this latest vision had symbols in it?" Mom inquired.

"Yeah," AJ said. She explained what she'd seen, about how the little robot had been poisoned.

"You said it was a rusty nail that poisoned the robot?" Mom said.

"I think so?" AJ said. "It wasn't a regular nail." She also explained why she was so out of it that day—reaching for that railroad spike, or whatever it was, had been pushing her powers too hard.

"Just a sec," Mom said, pulling out her phone. She quickly opened a note she'd taken. "You had me investigating someone last night. A Rusty Thomas, right?"

"I did," AJ said. "I was really suspicious about him. So I gave him to you, an unbiased third party, to crawl through his social media accounts. I would be searching for things that made him guilty. You wouldn't."

Mom gave her a bright smile. "That's my thinking girl. Rusty railroad spike. Rusty Thomas. That's a pretty strong connection."

"How?" AJ said, confused. The rusty part she got.

"Thomas the Tank Engine?" Mom said. "It's a character. It was a really popular cartoon when you were growing up."

"Oh, I remember," Bea said. "That boy who lived down the street from us. Darren? He was really into the whole thing. He even had Thomas the Tank Engine PJs."

AJ vaguely remembered what Bea was talking about. As neither she nor Bea had been into trains or cars, they hadn't gotten those toys. Not that their mom would have allowed those sorts of things—girls got dolls. Particularly her mom's princesses.

"So I think it's pretty obvious that your vision showed you who the killer is," Mom said, sounding smug. "The main question, is what are you going to do about it?"

Chapter Nineteen

Though breakfast and caffeine had helped AJ's headache, she still felt as though her brain were wrapped in cotton batting and trying to think through that was too hard.

Fortunately, she didn't have to solve this problem alone.

She left Bea and her mom brainstorming ideas for how to best catch Rusty, or discover some proof that he was the killer, while she walked down Main Street to the competition area. They had come up with a few things that she was going to put into motion that morning, though much of the plan was still amorphous at best.

Two women sat at the opening to the tent where the meats would soon be turned in for the competition. Inside, several of the LCBA people as well as the Milltown committee were standing around. The tables were still all set up, the chairs congregated around them, and everything looked clean.

One of the first people AJ saw was Fred Hanson. He wore his usual flannels, jeans, and work boots. He took one look at her then took her gently by the arm and led her over to the table where a coffee urn, cups and accessories stood waiting.

"I've already had a lot of coffee," AJ grumbled as they stood in line behind two others set to get their fix.

Fred shot her a look. "Not enough."

AJ snorted but didn't deny it.

"So tell me, what has my muse been up to that has her looking so drawn and haggard?"

Even though AJ still didn't feel like it, she found herself smiling. Fred's insistence that she was his muse at first had flummoxed her, but now she found it endearing.

"There might have been a vision involved," AJ said in such a quiet voice that Fred had to lean closer to her to hear her.

"Really?" he purred. "What delightful details can you share?"

"Well," AJ said, starting off a bit louder so that other people could hear, "you're aware that people are falsely accusing Lili Jang of poisoning Bob Woodward?"

"I am," Fred said, nodding.

A feeling of relief swept over AJ. That she wasn't having to prove Lili's innocence to Fred meant a lot to her. Either Fred knew something, or he was one-hundred percent willing to believe AJ's word on the matter.

"She had to withdraw from the competition. Someone tampered with her sauces yesterday, and she doesn't want to accidentally hurt anyone," AJ continued. "It's such a shame. I think she was poised to take the title this year. Be the grand champion."

"Interesting," Fred said. "Do you think the motivation for targeting her might be jealousy?"

"Professional envy, yes," AJ said firmly.

"It's a real shame, though, that no one is going to have the opportunity to taste her BBQ this weekend," Fred said.

"We might on Monday," AJ said. This was one of the ideas that her mom and Bea had thrown out. Have a big picnic Monday at noon, to thank the contestants and somehow get Rusty to show his hand there. "Maybe have a locals-only BBQ picnic." The LCBA was also having a picnic at the same time, catered by Sandy's. The two events could be separate, but AJ assumed that people might walk from one to the other and back.

"Sounds lovely," Fred said. They reached the front of the line and Fred started pouring AJ a cup of coffee, automatically adding two sugars and three creams to it before handing it to her.

"Bless you, thank you, bless you," AJ said as they walked away and let the next people in line serve themselves.

"But that isn't why you look so rundown," Fred said quietly as they walked over to an empty corner of the tent.

"No," AJ admitted. She told him about her vision, how she thought Lili was in danger of being poisoned.

She emphasized that it was a rusty railroad spike that she'd seen, then ignored the way that Fred's eyes lit up at the reference.

He could draw his own conclusions. Possibly he'd had a set of Thomas the Tank Engine PJs himself.

At the end of her tale, AJ added, "So, could you spread it around that you're looking for this sort of clue? I don't know how you'd phrase it, to leave me and my visions out of it. But I'd still like other people looking and thinking about how Lili is being targeted, how a rusty railroad spike might be involved."

"You got it," Fred said with a certain gleam in his eye.

Though Fred wasn't as involved in the town's gossip as he used to be—he was actually writing books these days and not just sitting around and talking about writing—he still had a reputation. Everyone, AJ included, thought of him first when it came to finding out what was happening in Milltown, that is, if the information wasn't on the Milltown app.

Telling what she could to Fred was the best way she knew to spread the word, to make sure that people would learn about the possible involvement of Rusty Thomas.

Katrice Freeman, one of the LCBA members, walked over to talk with AJ about how the contest was doing. She was a large African-American woman, as tall as AJ but easily twice as wide, with ample curves and hips. She wore her hair puffed out in a stylish Afro, with pinkish-purple eye makeup that matched her pretty pink-and-gray blouse. Though she was from Alabama, her accent came and went, depending on what she needed.

For now, Katrice greeted AJ with only a hint of a drawl, asking whether or not she'd be in the tent all day.

Fred drifted away from the pair of them, first having a quiet chat with Sandy, then Lionel, then others.

AJ kept her smile to herself about how the information was spreading as she told Katrice that yes, she would be there all day.

She might not have a complete plan for how to catch Rusty in the act. But she had agreed with Mom and Bea that they had to put pressure on him.

A part of AJ felt bad because she didn't have definitive proof that Rusty Thomas was, in fact, the killer. All she had was her interpretation of a vision.

Still, she wasn't going to the police and accusing him. No, she was doing something much worse: letting his peers judge him.

She knew that Gabby didn't think that Rusty had it in him to kill someone. But her mom disagreed, particularly given some of the nasty things Rusty had to say about Bob. She'd found some old blog posts that Rusty had done, detailing just how bitter he was about the entire reality TV show.

AJ had been impressed with how her mom had used the Wayback Machine in order to dig up those posts.

It was a good reminder that anything on the internet could, indeed, live forever.

The judges arrived soon after that. Most of them ignored the coffee stand, opting instead for water. AJ kind of understood that—they didn't want another strong taste to affect their palates. She helped get all the judges seated, making sure that every table had a captain at it.

Soon enough, it was noon, and the first of the meat boxes started getting turned in. The table captains were called to the door of the tent to collect the boxes and take them back to their tables.

First, he or she opened the box and presented the contents to the judges seated there.

AJ kept her sniggers to herself, how they made such a production of it, displaying the boxes like the best TV hosts with fancy prizes.

The boxes were white Styrofoam, with a bed of green parsley underneath the meat. Cecelia had tweezers that she used for placing the various pieces of greenery, to make sure that the box looked just right.

Then, each judge at the table got a piece of whatever was in the box. Chicken was first. The boxes had six pieces, either chicken thighs or chicken drumsticks. The heavenly smell of roasted meat filled the tent. AJ thought about the chicken that Elanor had decreed unworthy for the judges and wondered how in the world they were ever going to make a decision.

She understood that after appearance, the judges rated meat based on tenderness and taste. Most judges took a single bite, closing their eyes while tasting. Then they examined the meat.

"What are they doing?" AJ asked Katrice as she watched.

"The skin is supposed to be melted on, in terms of tenderness. If they can see teeth marks from their bite, it isn't tender enough," Katrice replied.

"Huh," was all that AJ had to say. She might have to take an LCBA judging class one of these days. It would mean spending a weekend in Seattle, or down in Portland, but it might be worth it. Particularly if she got to try some of the amazing meat that these BBQ teams produced.

"These are some well-trained judges," Katrice commented. "See how serious they all look?"

AJ nodded. She'd noted that the judges had all stopped smiling when the meat boxes had been brought in.

"They aren't supposed to give any visible reaction to a product, either good or bad. Don't want to influence the others at the table, even unconsciously," Katrice said.

"Fascinating," AJ said. "Is there any way to cheat? To figure out which team turned in which box?"

"Anything's possible," Katrice said with a shrug. "We do everything we can to make it difficult, though. Up front, a team turns in their box. One of the two people at the table there assigns each team a number and sticks the number on the box. There's a sheet of paper that matches the numbers to the boxes, but neither the captains nor the judges ever see those."

"A team could time their turn-ins, though, so that they were always number eleven, say," AJ pointed out.

"Not really, as the numbers continue to go up sequentially. They don't restart with each turn in. But someone could count so they would always be the eleventh one to turn something in," Katrice said. "However, the table captains aren't called up in the same order. It would be really difficult to make sure that the same captain always got the same box. Plus, the team wouldn't have to just bribe the captain. They'd have to bribe every judge at a table. And sometimes the judges get switched around from round to round. Not every contestant enters meat for every category."

AJ nodded. It would be very difficult for a team to

curry favor with a judge. Of course, the system wasn't perfect, but it looked like it would take a lot of effort to circumvent it.

Once all the chicken boxes were judged, and the rankings sent back to the front of the tent, the atmosphere in the tent changed abruptly. The judges took a break, stood up, chatted with other people at their table or with their friends. Suddenly, it was a friendly get together.

That lasted until the next product was turned in, and everyone grew serious again.

Ribs were also judged on tenderness, how well the meat pulled away from the bone. If it pulled too far away, the meat tended to be dry.

Brisket was given a wiggle test, to see how tender it was. Whereas the pulled pork was actually pulled apart as part of the judging.

"See that?" Katrice pointed at one of the pork boxes. In addition to a heap of pulled meat were some darker hunks. "Those are burnt ends. Pit master must be really confident in their product to turn those in."

"They're not required?" AJ asked. From where she was standing, she could see that only some of the boxes contained them, possibly fewer than half.

"Nope. Just the pulled pork. The ends need to be cooked so they're crispy, but not dry. Flavorful, full of the taste of the rub, but you still need to be able to taste the pork. They're tricky to get right."

Soon, all the meat had been judged and AJ could be on her way. It had been a fascinating interlude, learning all about the contest.

Now, she was ready to try some of that BBQ herself.

Chapter Twenty

AJ met her mom and Bea close to the entrance to the contestant area. They had their tickets in hand and were ready to follow her lead.

First, AJ walked over to Las Chicas de Carne, introducing Gabby, Elanor, and Cecelia to her mom and Bea.

"How'd everything turn out?" AJ asked Elanor.

"I feel confident about the brisket. And the pork," Elanor said. "Chicken's always impossible to judge. The ribs...I still think the ribs needed to cook a bit longer," she said, shooting a glare at Gabby.

Gabby shrugged. "Inez said they were done."

AJ shook her head slightly so neither Bea nor her mom would ask about who Inez was.

"Can we taste anything?" AJ said with a grin.

"Absolutely!" Cecelia said, coming over to talk with them.

She was the "face" of the group, and she looked amazing as always. AJ would never have skin that practically glowed that way. Though AJ was tall and athletically built, Cecelia made her feel small yet ungraceful.

AJ, Bea, and their mom all tried different meats, with AJ getting the brisket, Bea getting the pulled pork, and their mom trying the ribs.

Picnic tables had been set up in the center of the ring made by the contestants. They took their prizes over to one and settled in.

"O.M.G.," Bea said after taking a bite. "I can see why Elanor is confident about the pulled pork."

"And the brisket," AJ added after a moment. She tried gently shaking it as she'd seen the judges earlier, seeing how much wiggle the piece of meat had. It certainly seemed flexible to her, but she wasn't a judge. It was tasty. The sauce served with the meat enhanced the general "meatiness" of brisket, with a lovely smoky flavor underneath.

Mom didn't seem as impressed with the ribs, saying that they were slightly dry. Still, even she would admit that it was some of the best BBQ that she'd ever tried.

The three of them spent the next couple of hours trying many varieties of the different meats available, all agreeing that the judges had a horrible job, not because of the tasting, but because of how difficult it would be to choose a winner.

Finally, they made their way over to where Lili stood behind her smokers.

"Hey there," AJ called out as they approached. "How are you holding up?"

"I am well," Lili said gravely.

She didn't look too worried, or even depressed,

though it was difficult to tell, as always, given her deadpan expression.

"I sold four smokers this weekend," Lili added, pride touching her voice. "Even though I couldn't compete, the commissions will pay for the weekend."

"That's awesome!" AJ said, happy for her.

"We've been talking about doing a picnic on Monday," Bea said as she came to stand next to AJ. "Just for the locals. Do you think you could make something for it?"

Lili's eyes widened—quite a show of emotion, as far as AJ was concerned.

"Are you certain?" Lili inquired.

"Absolutely," Bea said firmly.

"I was already planning on buying all new spices and meat," Lili confided. "I just...I can't trust anything that I brought with me."

AJ knew that Lili was something of a germaphobe, and so even though her things were probably okay, it made sense to her that Lili would replace it all anyway.

"I won't be able to replace everything, though. Some of the more exotic spices I can only get at Asian supermarkets, and there isn't one in town. I checked," she added, turning accusing eyes toward AJ, as if she were to blame for this lack.

"Sorry, we're a small town," AJ said. "There is the Mexican cantina. They might have spices you haven't heard of."

Lili grew thoughtful. "Interesting. I may go exploring, there."

Mom suddenly piped up. "We may have a plan for

how to catch the person who's coming after you," she said quietly. "Can you pretend to be poisoned?"

Lili's eyes grew wide again. "I'm not good at acting. Or lying," she said. "It just...isn't in my nature."

Mom nodded. "I thought as much. We will plan accordingly."

AJ looked at Bea and Mom, though neither of them appeared to want to enlighten either her or Lili.

They said their goodbyes and wandered over to the next competitor while Lili started up her spiel for the customer wandering by.

"What do you have planned?" AJ asked quietly.

Mom gave her a mysterious smile. "Don't you worry about it. I think the picnic thing on Monday is a lovely idea. Bea, you be sure to invite Rusty, won't you?"

Bea rolled her eyes. "I'm not really a *femme fatale*, you know."

"No, but you're pretty and blonde. I'm pretty sure you can distract a man if you want to," Mom said, her tone even.

"Oh, all right, fine," Bea huffed. She pasted a cute smile on her face, something that AJ could tell wasn't real though most people wouldn't know the difference.

Then Bea stood up straighter and pulled her shoulders back.

AJ was suddenly aware that her sister was *much* more endowed than she'd ever be.

"I'll let the girls do the talking," Bea said, bouncing slightly.

"Be sure to invite Jack Jackson," AJ said. "And have him invite whoever he wants."

"Yes, yes," Bea said as she sauntered away.

"I always considered it such a good thing that Bea found Peter when she did," Mom commented. "So she never had to survive using her other assets, that she had someone in her corner."

AJ nodded. "Would have been interesting to see her hone those weapons of hers, though."

Mom gave a harsh laugh. "Oh, she already has. Trust me. Particularly when dealing with male customers or gallery owners. I haven't seen her work in this fashion very often, but every once in a while, like at an opening, she would go into full hunting mode. Like she is now."

"Huh," AJ said. She'd only made it to a few of Bea's art shows. She'd always been too busy working, something she was trying to make up for now.

"And what about you?" Mom said, turning to glance at AJ.

"What about me?" AJ said warily. Her head had definitely gotten better as the day had passed, but a headache still throbbed behind her eyes. She so didn't want to be forced into playing any of her mother's games. Not today.

Not ever, to be honest.

"Your skills have always been organization and team building," Mom said confidently. "So can I rely on you to set everything up for this picnic?"

AJ blinked. "Yes. This area will be cleaned first thing tomorrow morning, and available for us to use for a picnic. Do we need beverages? Or have people bring their own? How about plates, napkins, utensils?"

"We'll provide. Or maybe the inn will?" Mom said.

"I might be able to arrange that," AJ said slowly. As

Bob hadn't actually finalized any of arrangements for the LCBA meeting, Sandy had stepped up and volunteered, so the inn wasn't providing anything for them. She'd talked about it with Katrice that morning.

"Good," Mom said. "You organize that. I'll help Bea out by inviting people. It's sure to be an event that everyone will talk about."

"More so than this?" AJ asked, teasing as she indicated the surrounding tents.

"Please," Mom said dismissively. "This is a general event. Ours will be private. Invite only. Much more exclusive. Possibly exciting."

AJ wasn't sure she liked the sound of that, but before she could object, her mom had wandered off to cause trouble.

The afternoon wound down and the air took on a distinct chill. Storm clouds threatened but no rain came to spoil their gathering.

Eventually, five PM rolled around. The band had stopped playing around four and struck their set. Tables were brought up onto the stage and trophies were lined up across them. Seemed that they had arrived on time and Sandy hadn't had to go and personally purchase any, as she'd assured Bob Woodward.

The top ten in each category of meat were announced publicly. However, a team only got called up to the stage if they placed in the top five for one of the categories. In addition, trophies and prize money only went to the top three.

Las Chicas placed seventh in ribs and third in brisket, but didn't get called up to the stage for anything else.

Albert and Paulo of Smoking Good Q got called up for both pork and brisket, while Gilbert and the Ruling Quartet BBQ managed to snag a first for chicken, but didn't place even in the top ten for anything else.

Jack Jackson was in the top ten for every single category of meat, and won the Milltown Open grand championship because he had the most points for the entire contest. No one else who AJ had gotten friendly with won any of the other top prizes.

AJ tried not to feel too smug when she realized that Rusty and his crew hadn't been announced or called to the stage once.

Gabby and Las Chicas spent time congratulating the other teams. AJ wandered over to where Lili was standing, rapidly entering things into her phone.

Before AJ could ask, Lili told her, "I'm entering all the numbers into a database to do further analysis on later."

"Of course you are," AJ said. "I'm still sorry you couldn't compete this time."

Lili shrugged but didn't look up from her phone. "I might have placed in a few categories. I know that I'm better than some of the others who did."

"Next time," AJ said firmly.

That got Lili to look up. "Will there be a next time?" she asked quietly.

"If I have anything to say about it, yes," she said firmly. "Just stick close to Gabby and the others for the rest of the day, and tomorrow as well. We'll try to flush out the real killer at noon, tomorrow."

AJ knew that she sounded a lot more convinced than she actually was.

Hopefully, her mom and Bea knew what they were doing.

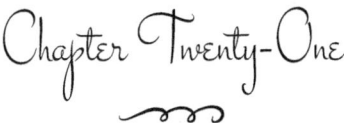

Chapter Twenty-One

The night passed without incident. No one else was poisoned, the police weren't called to attend any of AJ's friends. Gabby didn't text her about any strange encounters.

No, it was as if when the contest ended, so did all the threats.

The police were still interested in Lili as a possible suspect. However, they didn't have anything they could hold her on. They'd already let her know that she was free to go to the next contest.

Even the weather appeared to be cooperating. Though a squall had blown through, by morning, the sky was perfectly blue with a bit of bite to the air. There would be more rain that afternoon. AJ just knew it. Her headache was mostly gone but the pressure behind her eyes told her that the weather would stay nice for long.

AJ worked at the inn for much of the morning, helping with the Monday checkout rush. Everything had calmed down, though, by the time she needed to leave for the picnic.

All of the utensils, plates, napkins, and bottles of water provided by the inn had already been picked up by Bea and her mom. All AJ had to do was to get herself there on time.

It was a beautiful walk down Main Street to Sandy Point, where the picnic was being held. The Milltown Chamber of Commerce provided the space, allowing the LCBA to use the tent where the judging had taken place, while all the contestants had their picnic outside.

AJ was glad to see that everything was organized by the time she got down there. The main table was already overflowing with the offerings of the various BBQ participants.

Though Jack Jackson had (loudly) complained about having to feed a bunch of freeloaders, he still provided a heaping pile of brisket for people to eat. Albert and Paulo did Scotch eggs, while Lili did a large plate of hard-boiled eggs, sliced in half and filled with a spicy, creamy filling. Gilbert and crew provided thinly sliced, smoked ham with bread, Swiss cheese, and mustard. Las Chicas had taken their leftover chicken and simmered it all night in a mole sauce.

At least two dozen teams contributed, all of it lip-smacking, finger-licking good.

AJ was glad that the contest was over and that everyone was going to be leaving soon. Her waistline would thank her for going back to her usual diet. It was just that everything tasted so good and she had to try a bit of it all.

Rusty provided the dessert: a sweet vanilla custard that AJ had to grudgingly admit was good, particularly since he'd cooked it over a charcoal grill and that subtle hint of smoke enhanced all the other flavors.

The BBQ teams fell into talking with one another, all about grill times, temperatures, grades and cuts of meat, as well as where they'd be going next.

No one was buddying up to Rusty. It appeared that the whisper campaign was working. However, he was going to be leaving on Tuesday, and would be out of their reach.

Fortunately, people appeared to be genuinely accepting of Lili in their midst, particularly as Gabby pulled her into conversations. AJ found herself smiling when Lili almost became animated when talking about brisket.

AJ kept waiting for her mom or Bea to make some grand announcement. Maybe to make some sort of accusation of Rusty or someone else in the community.

Heck, maybe even convince Lili to pretend she'd been poisoned.

But the picnic went on without a hitch. The chairing committee from the LCBA came out of their tent toward the end and sampled what few leftovers remained, declaring that while Sandy had outdone herself with providing for them—savory stew and roasted clams—the other offerings were also really tasty.

AJ watched Mom engaging some of the contestants, questioning them about the death of Bob Woodward. However, it appeared that people wanted to put that behind them. She kept a pleasant smile on her face but AJ could tell that she was frustrated.

Whatever grand plan that she and Bea had worked out wasn't coming to fruition.

At the very end, AJ thanked everyone for coming, hoping to see them again the following year for the second annual Milltown Open.

After everyone had left, AJ, Bea, and their mom started cleaning up the remains of the picnic. They shooed off everyone else, telling them to go back to their trailers for the rest of the day.

Finally alone, AJ asked Bea in a quiet voice, "That was it? Nothing else planned? No big announcement or something?"

Bea gave her a sweet smile. "Oh, there's something else coming up. Just you wait."

AJ rolled her eyes. "Swell. Can you at least tell me about it? Give me a heads up?"

Bea glanced over both shoulders, making sure they were alone, before she said anything. "We were trying to stir up something for this picnic. Mom put herself out there specifically. But no one wanted to talk about Bob's death. Fortunately, we had an alternative plan for that."

She paused and nodded toward their mom. "Should have seen the look of relief on Rusty's face when Jack Jackson said we shouldn't be talking any more about it. Mom told me to watch for Rusty. Glad I did."

AJ nodded, impressed with her mother's prowess, but not surprised. "Yeah, Mom knows how to manipulate people, that's for certain. What was this all for, then?"

"To make sure that we had the right person," Bea

said. "And to lay a trap for this evening. Lili is joining us for dinner. She'll be alone, away from Gabby and the others. If someone is going to do something to her, we've now set up the perfect time."

"All right," AJ said, nodding. "But if she's going out to dinner with us, how will he poison her?"

"He's going to kidnap her on the way to the restaurant," Bea said, beaming.

AJ rolled her eyes. "Gabby said that Rusty was too lazy to do much of anything. It's why she doesn't believe that he's the killer. Plus, going from poisoning to kidnapping is a *huge* step. Why would he do that, when he can just wait until the next contest? Bide his time?"

"Because Lili's going to be walking to the restaurant," Bea said, beaming at her. "And you remember that stretch of highway that's so dangerous for pedestrians?"

AJ slowly nodded. That particular chunk of 101 was listed in the top ten—and occasionally in the top five—most dangerous highways in all of the US. There were just a few other places along the coast that were as deadly and had so many pedestrian deaths.

"So perhaps Lili has an 'accident' along that stretch," Bea said.

"How do we stop that from happening?" AJ said, perplexed. "Particularly if Lili is walking on her own?"

"You'll be right behind her!" Bea said proudly. "You'll be wearing all black. No one will see you."

"How am I supposed to stop a moving vehicle?" AJ said, exasperated. Sure, she had some magic. Not enough to stop a car.

"I'm sure you can figure something out," Bea said.

"What? No," AJ said. How was she supposed to figure out how to prevent someone from smashing into Lili in their car?

"How about I offer to drive Lili?" AJ said. "That way, if someone tries to attack her, at least I'll be there to help."

Bea shook her head. "No, Rusty is too much of a coward. Mom told him about the road. Then, later, invited Lili to dinner while Rusty was in earshot. We'd already warned Lili about the ruse. She insisted that she'll walk there alone."

"The weather isn't going to cooperate," AJ said. "It's going to be raining heavily. No one is going to want to walk in that."

"So that will make it even easier to dodge an oncoming car," Bea told her smugly.

"This plan is stupid," AJ said. "Either Lili's going to get killed, or I am. Or possibly both of us."

"We could follow you as well, in a car," Bea said slowly. "To make sure that you both get to the restaurant safely."

"Completely soaking wet as well," AJ grumbled.

"You can dry yourself off," Bea pointed out.

At least she had a point with that. AJ's magic did allow her to control the water that way, to send it flowing away from her after getting soaking wet.

And though she could form a shield out of the water, it wasn't strong enough to stop a bullet, let alone a moving vehicle.

"Are you certain that Rusty is going to come after Lili

like this? I mean, wouldn't a hit and run accident look kind of bad?"

"Not if he isn't caught," Bea said. "Plus, maybe he claims that she ran into traffic, into his car, and 'finds' a suicide note on her?"

AJ sighed. While she agreed that Rusty was probably the killer—the feeling had been growing on her during their picnic—she still didn't think this was the best way to try to trap him.

"And what about Roland?" AJ said. "He's supposed to come to dinner too."

"Uhm, he can walk with you?" Bea suggested, finally sounding uncertain of the entire ridiculousness.

"He's not going to be happy about this either," AJ grumbled.

There had to be a better way, other than walking along the most dangerous stretch of 101.

"How about instead we all drive like sane, sensible people to the restaurant. Rusty won't be able to come in and check on is. Maybe Lili forgets something in the car. Has to go back into the parking lot by herself. He can scoop her up then. And I'll be waiting for him," AJ said.

"I don't know. She said she'll be walking," Bea pointed out.

"Yes, and if the weather really is as nasty as I think it's going to be, she can drive herself. Maybe something goes wrong with her car in the parking lot," AJ suggested.

Bea heaved a heavy sigh. "I really think it would be easier for Rusty, or anyone, to attack her while she's alone on the road."

"And I keep telling you that's an insane plan and doomed to fail," AJ said stubbornly.

"She isn't agreeing to it, is she?" Mom said as she suddenly appeared beside them.

"No," Bea scowled. "You were right."

"So what's the real plan?" AJ said, glaring from to the other.

It was only slightly better than the one she'd been told about. She might still get soaking wet, but at least she wasn't going to be walking along a dangerous highway late at night.

No, just stuck in a parking lot, waiting for a killer to strike.

Chapter Twenty-Two

The rain appeared soon after AJ got back to the inn. Generally, she didn't mind the water, or being wet. But this rain had a mind of its own. The cold was trying to seep into her bones and her headache rebloomed, making it difficult to think.

Despite that, AJ still sat at her desk for a while that afternoon, trying to see if she could have a vision about later that evening. Nothing came to her. She even talked with Gabby for a while, to see if she had any sense of something coming, but she didn't either.

Either Rusty wasn't going to try anything, or they'd foil him, so there wasn't anything to worry about.

AJ left her phone turned on, next to her, while she worked at her desk, seeing if perhaps Carla, the ghost of the other psychic, would show up and warn her, one way or another. But Carla remained silent as well. AJ hadn't heard much from the ghost since AJ had caught her killer three months before. Though according to Gabby, Carla had reached out to her, brought her to Milltown.

Maybe Carla was now done with AJ, and wouldn't show up again.

Somehow, AJ doubted that would be the case.

Finally, it was time to go to dinner. AJ scurried through the rain to her place, where she put on a much nicer dress and makeup. At least she didn't look completely haggard, even after working all day. That was a definite change for her, putting in so few hours and not being drained of life by her work.

Almost as if she had a life or something.

The dress she chose was long-sleeved and various shades of black and gray, the opposite of springy or summery. However, she felt as though she needed to be dressed like a shadow so she wouldn't be easily seen when skulking around a dark parking lot.

Just at five thirty, Roland knocked on the door.

AJ loved seeing him so dressed up, in a nice blue shirt with a collar of white, a dark gray suit, and a gold-colored tie. He cleaned up well, though his big beard did make him look more like a hipster than a businessman.

"Hi, you," AJ said, drawing Roland in for a long hug.

He smelled like the wood and plants he worked with, along with a hint of something sweeter. He felt solid in her arms, warm and steady, someone she could rely on.

"It's good to see you," AJ said, still wrapped around him.

"Good to see you as well," Roland murmured into her hair. "What little I can see of you," he added, teasing.

"It's been a weekend, let me tell you," AJ said, finally drawing back.

"What are you worried about?" Roland asked, taking in her expression.

AJ sighed. "Everything. We still haven't caught the killer. My sister and my mom have this plan for tonight, thinking they're going to catch him. I think they're crazy. He's just going to wait until he has an easier opportunity than this."

"Okay," Roland said slowly. "Want to tell me about it?"

"While we drive to the restaurant, sure," AJ said. She locked up her house and walked with him to the car. The rain had calmed down and settled into a heavy mist, though that wasn't much better in terms of the cold.

AJ told Roland of the first plan, walking to the restaurant, and how stupid that would have been. Now, though, she was supposed to hide somewhere, in her good dress and shoes, hoping that this idiot tried to take advantage of Lili while she was going into the restaurant.

At least Gabby had agreed to the plan, and was going to light a fire under Rusty's ass. AJ wasn't sure how Gabby was going to get him motivated, but she trusted that the fire witch would be able to figure it out.

"He won't show. Not before dinner," AJ said. "I just know it."

"You know it?" Roland asked. "Or you *know* know it?"

"I haven't had a vision about it, if that's what you're asking about," AJ said. "If he tries anything, it will be after dinner. When the parking lot is a lot more empty, and he has a better chance of catching Lili alone. And no one will be expecting her anywhere."

"You know, a guy could develop a complex if his date keeps getting kidnapped in parking lots when they go out," Roland said.

AJ heard the worry under his light-hearted words.

"At least this time, you'll know where I'm going and what I'm facing," AJ pointed out.

"Will I?" Roland asked. "Or will you just vanish again?"

"The point is to stop Rusty *before* he grabs Lili, to catch him in the act this time," AJ said.

Roland sighed. "I know she's your friend. And that you're worried about her. But I get to worry about you, okay?"

"Okay," AJ said, reaching her hand across the center console and clasping his oh-so-delightfully-warm hand resting in his lap.

"You're really cold," Roland said.

"Normally, the hormones keep me warmer than usual," AJ said. "But there's just something in the air tonight, some sort of chill that I can't seem to shake."

"Are you coming down with something?"

AJ gave a deliberate swallow to see if her throat was sore. A swollen throat was generally her first sign of illness.

Nope. Throat felt fine. Her head hurt, but that was still from the other day. And the constantly changing weather.

"I'll be fine," AJ assured Roland, pleased that he cared enough to be worried.

"And I'll do what I can to make sure you stay that way," Roland replied.

"Thank you," AJ said. "For caring. For being a part of this craziness. And for meeting my mother."

"You ever figure out what's really going on with her?" Roland asked.

"Bea thinks something happened to one of her friends, like cancer. At this point, she would have told us if there was something seriously wrong with her personally."

"Would she?" Roland asked. "Or would she wait until afterward? My mother wrote me a letter that deliberately didn't arrive until after she went in for surgery."

AJ felt her eyes go wide. "Wow. No, my mom wouldn't do that. What was wrong with your mom?"

"She had some sort of breast cancer. They were able to cut it out. Double partial mastectomy. She didn't have chemo or radiation afterward. Just went on as if nothing had happened," Roland said.

"I promise I will communicate more than that?" AJ said, unsure what else to say.

That got her a quick squeeze of her fingers. "Thanks. And it's good to know that your mom wouldn't do that to you."

"I don't think she would. She's more of a martyr," AJ said. "She needs more attention than that."

That got her a snort of amusement.

AJ looked around the parking lot of the restaurant when they arrived. The building itself was to her right, down a long walkway, perched on a short cliff looking out over the ocean. A thick row of trees kept the noise and lights from the highway, making the area seem darker and more isolated than she would have expected. She was barely able to see the white stripes neatly demarcating the parking spots.

The rain had picked up slightly, and AJ felt soft drops on her hair. It chilled her as much as if cold water was trickling down her neck.

Yes, this *could* be the perfect place for a kidnapping. But it was still too bright.

"You go on inside. I want to check something out," AJ told Roland. She waited until he'd turned away before she hiked across the parking lot to one of the lights that edged it. A single car sat just beyond the circle of light, crouching in the darkness: Lili's car.

AJ reached out to touch the light pole. The sodden wood instantly soaked her fingers, and she grimaced at the feeling of slimy moss against her skin.

Given the amount of rain falling, it didn't take much to direct an onslaught of water to the head of the light, pushing it into the sealed compartment.

She couldn't work with fire, or electricity. Water, though, was her friend. And it could find its way into *anything*, given time and a slight push.

The light began to sputter and hiss.

AJ turned and started walking back toward the building, allowing herself a satisfied grin when the light behind her blinked out before she was halfway across. She pushed the water away from herself, drying herself off, so that by the time she reached the walkway she was mostly dry.

Crap.

Roland hadn't continued on into the restaurant as she'd asked. He'd stopped, and was standing on the walkway, waiting for her.

"Did you know that light was just about to go out?" he inquired as they made their way to the door of the restaurant.

"I had a feeling about it," AJ told him. She knew that she needed to tell him about her magic one day.

However, today was not that day.

When they walked into the building, Roland shot her another strange look. "Are you dry?" he asked as he took her coat from her, handing it over to the old man standing behind the coat check.

"I must have just walked between the raindrops," AJ said lightly.

Dang it! He wasn't supposed to notice that she'd dried herself off. She gave him a bright smile.

"Okay," Roland said slowly.

Their table was ready for them. As Roland had made the reservation, and used his family's name, he'd managed to get them a table close to the windows looking out over the ocean, to watch the sunset, though AJ doubted that there was a bad seat in the entire place.

Floor to ceiling windows lined two of the four walls. They'd been covered in some sort of polarizing film, so it was like looking outside wearing some sort of shades. Dark clouds filled the horizon, and AJ could just barely make out the water.

They'd have to come back here in the summer, when they could actually watch a sunset.

The tables all had heavy linens on them, with modern, minimalist glassware and utensils. Leather folders encased the menus, and the wine menu was easily as long as the food menu. Smells of garlic and lemon permeated the air, making AJ's mouth water.

She'd had so much good food this weekend! She was going to have to go swimming more than once this week to make up for it.

Lili was already seated at the table, and gave them a shy hello. She wore her usual peach-colored shirt, though this one was long-sleeved and not a T-shirt, with black dress pants. She explained that she'd arrived early and sat in her car in the parking lot for a while, but as no one else had parked close to her, she'd gone into the restaurant.

Mom and Bea came in shortly afterward. Bea wore her usual style of boho blousy shirt, this time covered in pink flowers outlined in thin strips of silver, over a silvery-gray skirt. If AJ had tried to pull off such an outfit she would have looked like a secretary who worked for a government office. Instead, Bea made it look artistic.

Irene Steward, of course, was wearing an incredibly chic pantsuit, the color a purple-gray that seemed both somber yet festive. Her pewter-colored blouse was pure silk and probably tailored within an inch of its life, so it fit her mom exactly.

Bea and Mom carried most of the conversation that evening, though Mom did get in a few questions about Roland, urging him to tell his story.

Roland didn't go into his personal history much, about being raised by two lawyers and how they'd expected him to carry on the family tradition. Instead, he talked about running a successful lawn-care business that was seasonal, so that he had the opportunity to continue his studies as a historian during the winters.

"Historian? How fascinating," Mom commented, though AJ could tell it wasn't something she was interested in at all.

No, Mom was always looking forward, not backwards. It might be part of why AJ had so much difficulty looking into the past of her clients, why it was so easy for her to look into the future as well.

Food for thought.

Though Lili didn't say much, AJ could tell that she was having a good time. They took their time ordering various courses, trying different wines, chatting, laughing, and sharing stories.

By the time they were having coffee, port, or other after dessert drinks, it was nearly nine PM and they were the last diners in the restaurant, which apparently closed soon.

Lili finally figured out that they were about to leave, to see if someone was awaiting her in the parking lot. She grew stiffly silent before she started staring woodenly at AJ.

AJ nodded at her when there was a break in the conversation. "Yeah, let's go hit the restroom before we leave," she told Lili directly.

Lili nodded and stood, following her to the brightly lit bathroom.

"Are you ready?" AJ asked Lili quietly.

"I am," Lili said, nodding. "Are you sure he's out there?"

"Gabby texted me during dinner to let me know that he drove away and left his camp," AJ told her. "So he's certainly someplace."

"Okay," Lili said. "I parked at the far end of the parking lot."

"I saw. I'll be right behind you when you leave," AJ assured the other woman.

She couldn't stop a bullet with her water.

But she could certainly stop a man, if need be.

"Let's go," Lili said.

"Now?" AJ asked, a little taken aback. She'd planned on going back into the restaurant to say goodbye to everyone.

"Yes," Lili said firmly. "Before I change my mind."

"I'm following you, then," AJ said.

She knew that Roland would be a little angry with her for just taking off.

However, there wasn't anything he could do to protect her.

No, Lili and AJ were going to face Rusty alone.

And take him down.

Chapter Twenty-Three

AJ didn't bother trying to collect her coat from the coatroom at the front of the restaurant. Her black dress had long sleeves, and she would use the rain to help her hide.

Lili walked out boldly, almost robotically.

AJ counted to ten slowly before she followed the other woman out into what turned out to be a pretty solid downpour.

The water drenched her instantly, turning her skin icy. At least that persistent headache of hers retreated in the cold, instead of blooming. It had grown very dark, but Gabby had taught AJ the trick of seeing with the rain, not with light.

It still took AJ some time to make the switch, to sensing what was happening instead of seeing it. Her senses showed her half a dozen cars still in the parking lot: Roland's, Bea's, probably a couple that belonged to the staff, and two parked on the far edge.

One of which belonged to Lili.

Was the other, that was parked right behind it, Rusty's?

AJ stuck to the shadows and let the rain swallow her. She encased herself in the feel of the cold water so that she became just another part of the downpour.

She shivered and hurried across puddles in the asphalt.

A quiet gasp, followed by a thud, reached her ears.

AJ ran toward the two cars sitting in the dark.

The rain revealed a tall fat man standing beside the open door of a van.

Rusty.

"What are you doing?" AJ yelled, making her voice heard.

"Where did you come from?" Rusty said, starting.

Only then did AJ notice the gun in his hand.

"It was only supposed to be her. Jeez," Rusty said, shaking his head.

The hand holding the gun still pointed at her center mass, never wavering.

"Get in," he told her, gesturing toward the open door of the van.

AJ glanced over, seeing a crumpled shape on the floor.

"You didn't shoot her, did you?" AJ said.

"Of course I didn't," Rusty snapped. "She'd going to poison herself. And you. Now move."

"No," came a voice from beside AJ.

Crap, crap, and double crap.

Roland was there as well.

"What, are you all coming to get me?" Rusty said. "Like all of the BBQ teams? Like what that witch Gabby told me?" He paused, then added, "Although, this might work out well. Lover's tiff between you two. Completely unrelated deaths. Now, get in the van."

AJ wasn't about to comply. She had enough water to work with.

And she had to stop this.

No matter what Roland might see.

"I'm sorry," AJ told Roland.

He gave her a questioning look, obviously confused about what she was apologizing for.

Rusty took a step toward them, looking as though he was going to rush them, to push them into the van.

AJ stepped back into the puddle her rain-sense told her was there. Then she used the side of her foot to kick up a spray of water up toward Rusty.

She'd been working a lot with her water magic since Gabby had come into town, and was able to split the outgoing wave into two parts.

One thin, strong stream struck Rusty directly on the wrist, pushing the arm holding the gum above his head.

The sound of the gunshot echoed loudly.

The second, larger chunk of water plowed into Rusty's ample belly, striking him with as much force as a water cannon. He folded in half as he flew off his feet, landing at least a yard away, dropping the gun. The sound of his head hitting the asphalt made a thud.

AJ raced over to the prone man, directing more water at him. She wasn't going to drown him. Not exactly. Just knock him out so he stopped being a threat.

When Rusty's eyes rolled back in his head, AJ finally

looked up, over at Roland, who stood with his mouth open.

Crap.

Seemed like today *was* the day that she was going to have to tell him about her magic.

"Call the police," AJ directed him while she walked back over to the van to check on Lili.

The other woman lay on the floor of the van groaning, trying to shake off whatever Rusty had done to her. (AJ learned later that he'd struck her behind the head, on the back of the skull. It wasn't enough to render her unconscious, but it did daze her enough that he could push her into the van.)

Police sirens cut through the rain as AJ helped Lili sit up.

Roland still stood there, staring hard at AJ.

He reached out one hand and touched her hair.

"Still dry," he commented, almost to himself.

"We'll talk later," AJ assured him. "After you tell the police how *you* rescued the pair of us."

Roland looked at AJ, glanced over to where Rusty still lay, then gave her a grim nod. "Yeah. I see your point."

He deliberately turned his back to her then, standing in the rain with his arms crossed over his chest as the bright red-and-blue lights of the police cars came racing up.

Chapter Twenty-Four

The police found the suicide note that Rusty had written for Lili. They also got a quick confession out of him.

Seemed that Rusty had poisoned Bob, but not how anyone had imagined. The autopsy report (which came in a few days later) confirmed that Bob had died of a massive heart attack.

Rusty admitted to crushing up four ibuprofen and adding those to the orange-flavored mead he'd given Bob. Bob had complained about the mead being a bit bitter, but had drunk the entire bottle anyways.

Someone else had spiked Bob's gloves with a slower poison, an herb that was turning his fingers bright blue. Rusty was adamant that he hadn't done that, and no one else came forward to admit it.

AJ had her suspicions about Gilbert. However, there wasn't anything she or Gabby could do about him, except to watch him for now.

Roland took all the credit for stopping Rusty. He was very convincing about how he'd grown worried about AJ when she hadn't come back from going to the restroom, so he'd gone out to the parking lot to see if she was there. He'd even managed to joke about having lost his date once and being determined not to let it happen a second time.

Officer Brendan and Officer Naomi took him at face value and didn't question him too closely. Then again, Roland had studied law, and so knew exactly what he should and shouldn't say to the police.

Mom left Tuesday morning, though she'd promised (threatened?) both AJ and Bea that she'd return soon.

It wasn't until Tuesday night that Roland and AJ were able to meet and talk about what had happened, what he'd seen, what AJ had actually done.

AJ waited nervously for Roland at her house. He would believe her, she was pretty certain. There wasn't any trick to what she was doing. Or rather, the trick was magic.

Would he forgive her for not telling him about it sooner? Would he break up with her? Would he demand to know everything she could do and need for her to show it to him?

Or would he be more like Bea, who knew that her magic existed and would just as soon pretend that it didn't?

Roland knocked on AJ's door promptly at seven. He wore his usual work clothes, heavy black, white, and red flannel over tough cargo workpants and even tougher boots. His hair was still wet, probably from taking a shower after sweating all day.

He smelled good, but he didn't pull her into a hug, merely gave her a nod as he entered.

That hurt, but AJ was determined to forgive him.

She led him to her reading room, where her scrying bowl sat, already full of sparkling clean water. She put him in a chair beside her instead of across the table, which was where she sat clients.

"Do you want me to start?" AJ said. "Or do you have questions, first?"

Roland thought about that for a few moments. "You first."

"Okay," AJ said. She took a deep breath, then dipped her hand into the water, raised her hand, and let the water flow from her fingers.

"I'm a water witch," she said simply.

She scooped out a second palmful of water, only this time, when she raised her hand, the water didn't flow from her fingers. Instead, it drizzled down, more like sand than water. When the water reached the bowl, it piled up, like ice.

"Water is my element," AJ continued. She reached down and drew up a spike of water, molding it like clay. "I can do things with water. Lots of things," she said. She now used both her hands, lifting up some water between her two palms. Then she moved her hands away and the water stayed in the air, where she'd placed it, held up by a now solid spike of water rising from the bowl.

She finally looked up from her scrying bowl over at Roland.

His eyes were comically wide and his mouth had

fallen open. It took him a few moments to tear his eyes away from the display of her power to her face.

"This—" he paused, clearing his throat, "this isn't a new power, is it?"

"No, it isn't," AJ said. "But I didn't want to tell you about it. I didn't feel like it was time yet."

Roland nodded slowly. "But you were planning on telling me?"

"I knew I would have to tell you eventually," AJ admitted. "I didn't want to force the issue, though. Or our relationship."

"That...that makes sense," Roland said. "It's part of why you were always so insistent that we move slowly, isn't it? Because you knew that at some point, you'd have to show this to me. That we'd have to have this conversation."

"Exactly," AJ said. Feelings of relief, as well as additional nervousness, washed over her.

"So, what do you think?" AJ said after a moment. She pushed at the water, making it all drop back down into the bowl. "Can you forgive me for lying to you and not telling you about this?"

Roland took a deep breath. "I think so. You had to forgive me for lying to you at the start of our relationship. I was trying to protect myself, so you wouldn't think badly of me. You've just been doing the same. Only for longer."

"I think my secret was a little bigger than yours," AJ pointed out.

Roland snorted and nodded. "Ya think?"

He grinned at her, then slowly slid his hand across the table.

AJ relaxed as she gripped his warm fingers in hers.

"I'm not saying we're good yet," Roland warned. "We're going to have to talk about this more. And I'm going to have to take a minute to get used to the idea that my girlfriend is a witch." He gave her a grin. "Opens up a whole new avenue of historic study, though."

AJ just rolled her eyes. "Thank you for being willing to lie for me, though," she said.

Roland grew very serious again. "I didn't like doing that," he admitted. "That didn't feel good. But I would do it all again, in a heartbeat, to protect you. And your secret." He paused, his fingers twitching in hers for a moment. "Who else knows?"

"Only Bea," AJ said. "And she doesn't like it much. She pretends that I don't have magic, that all I can do is have visions."

"I can't do that," Roland said. "Not and have a close relationship with you. But your mom doesn't know?"

AJ snorted. "I wasn't about to tell her about my visions. But Bea did."

"Think she knows already? That you have magic?" Roland asked.

"God, I hope not," AJ said. She shuddered. She'd already veered so far from the life that her mom had envisioned her having. She wasn't about to admit to more.

Not unless she had to.

"So tell me about it," Roland said. "Start from the top."

And AJ did. When she got to the part about the first time she'd been shot at, by Irv, she'd taken him upstairs and the pair of them snuggled together in her bed as she finished her story, how she'd fought and foiled other killers, how she practiced using the fountain in her backyard and so on.

They fell asleep like that, curled up around each other. It wasn't the first time they'd slept in the same bed together, though it hadn't happened that often.

In the morning, AJ semi-woke up enough to find Roland reaching for her, and she gratefully settled her head on his shoulder, his warm arms around her.

"You okay?" she whispered after a while, sensing that he was still awake, his eyes open, staring at the bedroom ceiling.

"I think so," Roland said. "Didn't sleep a lot last night. Just kept thinking about things. What you are. What you can do." He paused, then asked, "Are there other witches?"

"I may know of a few," AJ said, hesitatingly. "But I'm not about to tell you who they are. It's like...it's like being gay, in the closet, okay? Not fair to tell you without their permission. They need to come out to you themselves."

"Fair enough," Roland said, nodding. "Just—is it half the town?"

AJ chuckled. "No. There might be one or two people in town. If that."

"All right," Roland said, relaxing. "I was getting worried for a moment, wondering if I needed to be more careful around my clients. Wouldn't do for me to be accidentally rude to someone who can fry my insides with just a glance."

AJ rolled her eyes. "No, most people are completely normal. I have no idea how many people have enough magic to matter, but I suspect the number's around one in a million."

That might have been an exaggeration. Gabby had placed the number lower, more like one in half a million. Still, AJ wanted to reassure Roland and there really wasn't any way of knowing for certain.

"I can tell when someone else does actual magic," AJ assured Roland. "And some things that seem like magic actually aren't." She told him about Gilbert, and his ability to turn his charisma up to eleven at will.

"He was able to do something, but it wasn't magic. Or at least not any magic that I can recognize," AJ said at the end of her story.

Just then, her alarm went off. With a groan, AJ reached over to shut it off.

"I need to get to work," she told Roland with regret.

"I should have left an hour ago," he admitted.

"We'll talk later?" AJ asked.

"We will," Roland said. He gave her a light peck that quickly grew in passion. "Among other things," he said teasingly.

"I'll hold you to that," AJ said as she slipped away from the bed, claiming the first shower of the morning.

She wasn't naïve enough to think that she and Roland wouldn't have more bumps along the road. He was taking it all very well currently, but he was quite possibly going to freak out at some point.

However, she had faith that the pair of them could deal with it. Her admitting to magic hadn't driven them apart.

Hopefully, her magic never would.

Chapter Twenty-Five

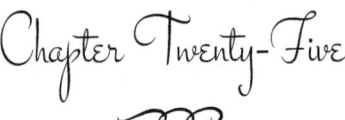

The rest of the week went smoothly enough for AJ, though she was busy seeing all the clients who she'd put off due to working the weekend at the BBQ competition. She and Roland stayed in close contact, with frequent texts and an occasional phone call.

Gabby and the crew of Las Chicas had headed out of town, driving to the next BBQ competition site further down the coast. AJ promised to stay in touch with the other witch, and Gabby promised to come back to visit at some point.

In addition, AJ promised to practice more with her water magic, particularly since she'd told Roland about it.

Gabby didn't want Roland to know about her, and AJ was glad that she hadn't mentioned the fire witch to him. He was just going to have to be patient when it came to meeting other people with magic.

The following Thursday, Bea texted AJ in the middle of the afternoon.

Moms come back. Get here for
diner and her announcement.

AJ rolled her eyes at the mis-spelling, but replied in the affirmative.

What in the world was their mother doing there? Why had she come back so soon? What was going on?

AJ knew that Bea would have said something more if she knew, so she didn't bother pestering her. She also didn't text her mom.

Mom would reveal all later that night, evidently.

The afternoon dragged on as AJ waited for dinner time to roll around. She sat in her office for a while using her farsense, to see if she could tell what was going on at the moment. However, while Gabby had assured AJ that she probably did have the ability to sense things like that, AJ still hadn't had any success with it.

No vision was impending either, the lights staying depressingly normal and didn't glow with some sort of portent.

When five PM finally rolled around, AJ hurried from the inn. At least the afternoon was nice, summer cautiously approaching. It wouldn't get really warm, though, until the fourth of July. Still, AJ was pleased to see the crowds on Main Street as she walked along. The town was thriving and that made her happy.

The steep hill up to Bea's neighborhood took its usual toll. AJ was still feeling the effects of eating so much good food the weekend before. She'd managed to get in a swim the previous day, and this weekend she'd get in a couple more.

Nothing seemed out of place along the cul-de-sac, all the eccentric houses still doing their own thing. Had the number of birdfeeders increased? Possibly. A flurry of birds took off as she approached. And the overgrown house was completely covered in bright new leaves.

AJ knocked, then walked into Bea's house, giving their usual greeting, "Hello! Burglars! Here to steal your stuff!"

"We're in here," Bea called out from the kitchen.

Huh. That was strange. She would have imagined that Mom and Bea would be ensconced on the couches in the living room, already halfway through their first bottle of wine.

Mom was standing behind the kitchen island, with an open laptop displaying a kite flying across it as the screen saver. Bea sat on the other side, with an empty chair beside her.

At least the wine was already open, and a glass was waiting for AJ.

Once AJ got herself settled, Mom took the stage.

"Now, I know you've both been worried about me. Even coming out and asking what the heck was going on, why was I here, in Milltown, for the first time," Mom started off with, glaring first at Bea, then AJ. "You were so worried you even asked if it had something to do with your father."

AJ and Bea nodded in synch. Yeap. They'd had more than one conversation about what had been going on.

"There's nothing wrong with me," Mom assured them. "I haven't come down with a deadly cancer or something else equally horrible and am about to keel over."

Though AJ had been fairly certain that was the case, an immense amount of relief washed over her when her mom said it. And AJ believed her. That wasn't the sort of thing that their mom might lie about.

"Do you remember my friend Samantha Gibbins?" Mom asked. "Ran the black-and-white gala and all the other fund raisers for the Denny Museum every year?"

AJ glanced at Bea, but she had an equally blank look on her face.

"Anyway, *she* was diagnosed with small cell lung cancer, even though she swears she never smoked," Mom said. "Maybe she just never inhaled. Anyway. It was six weeks from diagnosis to death." She paused and took a sip of her wine.

"That gave me something of a wake-up call," Mom continued.

AJ took a sip of her own glass of wine. That made sense. It was something she'd speculated about with Bea.

"So I decided to come down here, scout out the place," Mom said. "Spend more time with my children, because you never know how much time you have left."

"I'm glad you're okay," AJ said when Mom didn't continue right away.

"Is that your big announcement?" Bea asked.

Mom smiled brightly at them. "No, it isn't."

She turned the laptop around and brought it back to life before showing them the screen again. "While I appreciate your kind offer of always having your guest room at my disposal, Bea, I really need my own place. And I found one!"

AJ grew very still.

Crap.

That was a listing for a vacation house on the screen.

A listing that showed that it had just sold.

"So now I'll have my own place, and can come down to visit whenever I want!" Mom continued brightly. "I'm not moving down here permanently, but I think having a vacation cottage, like Bea's, is a good idea."

AJ and Bea exchanged a look. They were going to have so many words, so many opinions about this later.

"Where is it?" Bea asked, pulling the computer closer.

"It's the next neighborhood over," Mom said. She sounded a little put out. "There wasn't anything for sale in this cul-de-sac. And there's nothing close to your house, either," she added, glaring at AJ.

"Okay," AJ said, glancing at the screen. It was a small bungalow, built in the 1960s: a little cottage that had been updated with all the modern convivences, like AC, all new appliances, fresh paint and a new roof.

She'd always known her mom was financially well off. The divorce from their father had seen to that. Had she been saving toward some other home for a while? Or just cashed in some of her assets? Either way, AJ wasn't worried about Irene Steward suddenly being broke.

"That's so cool, Mom," Bea finally managed to say. "We'll be neighbors." She blinked a few times, then took a long drink of her wine.

"It will be nice to be able to see you more often," AJ

added thoughtfully as she pushed the laptop back toward Mom.

"Really, your display of enthusiasm is overwhelming," Mom said dryly.

"I do think it's a good idea," AJ said slowly. "It's just going to take some time to get used to it. Okay?"

Mom looked at her, then at Bea.

"Yes," Bea said obediently. "What AJ said. I look forward to seeing you more, but it's going to be odd at first."

That seemed to mollify their mom. "Really?"

"Yes, really," AJ said, reassuring her. "We have our own lives here. But I'm happy to make room for you as well. Maybe schedule a weekly dinner get-together or something."

Mom beamed at her. "That's exactly what I was thinking! Like every Sunday night."

"We'll see," AJ said, pulling back. "I'll need to work it out with my clients." She tended to take Sunday evenings off as she was generally exhausted after spending the day doing readings.

"Oh. Okay," Mom said, disappointed.

AJ smiled at her. "We *will* work something out," she reassured Mom. "I do want to see you. But I also have a schedule. And two jobs. And Bea has her painting. So we'll figure out a date and time that works for all of us. Okay?"

"All right," Mom said. She paused, then said, "You're both going to be good with this?"

AJ looked at Bea, who nodded.

"We are," AJ said firmly. "It'll be nice to have all the family who matter here in the same town."

"Cheers to that!" Mom said, holding up her wine glass.

AJ dutifully clinked glasses with both of them, then they each took a large swig.

Having their mom there in Milltown wouldn't be the worst thing in the world.

Right?

Read More!

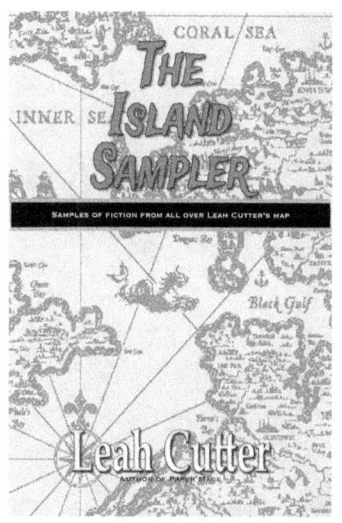

Do you enjoy exploring strange new worlds, new cultures, new people?

Journey into the various lands envisioned by Leah R Cutter.

Sign up for my newsletter and I'll start you on your travels with a free copy of my book, *The Island Sampler*.

http://www.LeahCutter.com/newsletter/

About the Author

Leah Cutter tells page-turning, wildly creative stories that always leave you guessing in the middle, but completely satisfied by the end.

She writes mystery of all sorts. Her Lake Hope cozy mysteries have been well received by readers, who just want to curl up and have tea with the main character. Her Halley Brown series, revolving around a private investigator who used to be with the Seattle Police Department, leave you guessing at every turn. And her speculative mysteries, such as the Alvin Goodfellow Case Files—a 1930s PI set on the moon—have garnered great reviews.

She's been published in magazines such as *Alfred Hitchcock's Mystery Magazine* and in anthologies like *Fiction River: Spies*. On top of that, Leah is the editor of the quarterly mystery magazine: *Mystery, Crime, and Mayhem*.

Read more books by Leah Cutter at www.KnottedRoadPress.com.

Follow her blog at www.LeahCutter.com.

Read more mysteries at www.MCM-Magazine.com

Reviews

It's true. Reviews help me sell more books. If you've

enjoyed this story, please consider leaving a review of it on your favorite site.

Come someplace new...
Do you enjoy exploring strange new worlds, new cultures, new people?

Journey into the various lands envisioned by Leah Cutter.

Sign up for my newsletter and I'll start you on your travels with a free copy of my book, *The Island Sampler*.

http://www.LeahCutter.com/newsletter/

Buy More!
Did you know that you can buy directly from the Knotted Road Press website?

https://www.knottedroadpress.com/shop/

About Knotted Road Press

Knotted Road Press publishes dynamic fiction set in exotic locations and unique non-fiction voices in genres such as autobiography, business, cookbooks, and how-to. Our authors cover a wide range of genres including science fiction, fantasy, mystery, literary, and poetry, appealing to all readers. We offer both DRM-free ebooks and print books for a global readership.

Knotted Road Press
www.KnottedRoadPress.com
www.KnottedRoadPress.com/Shop